BILLY DARE

Young B   Dare grows up fast when he
gets back   the homestead and finds his
mother ha been strangled by outlaws.
Determined   avenge her death, he learns
about tracking from an old army scout
and gets a retired gunfighter to teach him
how to handle a six-shooter. A professional
boxer gives him lessons in fist-fighting.
Billy sets out on his long search for the
outlaws. Before he reaches the end of his
vengeance trail, his new fighting skills are
tested to the utmost.

BILLY DARE

Billy Dare

by
Alan Irwin

Dales Large Print Books
Long Preston, North Yorkshire,
England.

British Library Cataloguing in Publication Data.

Irwin, Alan
  Billy Dare.

A catalogue record for this book is
available from the British Library

ISBN 1-85389-717-5 pbk

First published in Great Britain by Robert Hale Limited, 1990

Published in Large Print 1997 by arrangement with
Alan Irwin

Dales Large Print is an imprint of
Library Magna Books Ltd.
Printed and bound in Great Britain by
T.J. International Ltd., Cornwall, PL28 8RW.

To My Wife, Pat

1

Young Billy Dare checked his horse at the top of the rise, and looked down on the small homestead below, with its house and outbuilding, small corral and garden. From the small chimney on the house roof, a lazy plume of smoke spiralled slowly upwards.

This had been his home for the past twelve years, ever since, as a boy of six, he had arrived with his parents from the east. Billy had been born in Tennessee, but the lure of a bright future westward had brought his parents to East Texas. When they reached the spot where Billy's horse now stood, his parents Ben and Mary Dare had looked around and decided this was as far as they wanted to go.

Ben acquired a small piece of land in the valley, and they had settled happily there, and quickly adapted to the new environment. It had been a wise choice.

The soil was rich, and there was plenty of water in a small creek which ran through the property. Also, the valley was well sheltered from the cold north winds which blew down in the wintertime.

Things had gone well for them. Ben Dare was a strong, quiet man, with the determination and skill to get the best out of his land. He soon acquired a reputation for the quality of his crops, and the wad of banknotes hidden under the wooden floor of the house steadily increased in size over the years.

Billy had attended school in Larraby, a small town about four miles south. When he eventually left school, he helped his father out on the homestead.

Then, about two years ago, tragedy had struck when Ben mounted one of his horses one afternoon to ride into town. He was prepared for the mild spell of bucking usually indulged in by this particular animal, but not for the sudden breaking of a cinch, which caused him and the horse to part company. He fell awkwardly, and on the way down his head struck one of the stout posts surrounding the corral. It was a heavy blow. Then, as the horse lashed out at random with both hind legs, one hoof caught him on the forehead, just as he was falling away from the post to the ground. When his wife, who had seen the incident, reached him, he was unconscious. He died shortly after, in her arms.

Billy, who had been out riding on the pony given him on his last birthday, came home about an hour later. His mother was waiting for him at the door of the house. He rode up to her. From the look on her face, Billy sensed that something was amiss. To his consternation, she folded her arms around him.

'It's bad news, Billy,' she cried. 'Your pa took a fall from his horse near the corral there. I've covered him over with the blanket. He's dead, Billy. First help me to get him inside. Then ride into town, and tell Hank Osborne what's happened, and ask him to come and collect your pa as soon as he can.'

She broke down and sobbed. Billy

couldn't remember ever seeing his mother cry like that before, and what with seeing her that way, and realizing that his father was gone for good, he felt like a good bawl himself. He hugged his mother close for a while, then helped her to get his father inside. Then he jumped on his pony, and headed for town.

In the two years that had passed since the death of Ben Dare, Mary and Billy, both grieving in their separate ways, for Ben had been a good husband and father, carried on as they thought he would have wished. Billy was strong enough now to tackle any of the work required on the homestead, and he had learned enough to enable him to approach the high standards set by his father.

'You're a good boy, Billy,' Mary would tell him from time to time. 'Your pa would be proud of you.'

Billy was thinking of his father as he set off down the slope towards the house. He was returning from a trip he had made into town that morning to order seed, and carry out several other chores. There was no sign of his mother, which he thought was rather strange, because on a fine afternoon like this she was usually pottering around in the garden. He swung down from his horse.

'Hello, ma, I'm back,' he shouted. There was no reply.

He unsaddled the horse, and led it into the corral. Then he walked over to the house, entered, and stopped short. The table was overturned, and some broken crockery lay on the floor.

'Ma!' he shouted. There was no answer. He quickly went over to the bedroom door, pushed it open, and entered.

Mary Dare lay sprawled on the bed. She had a large purple bruise on each side of her jaw, and a red bandanna was twisted tightly around her neck. Her eyes were open in a fixed stare. Billy knew that she was dead. As he knelt on the bed beside her, he saw that a floorboard had been pulled up in the corner of the room, and an empty cash-box lay on the floor. He looked at the bruised and careworn face, distorted by the agony of strangulation. He reached over and gently loosened off the bandanna, then took his mother's hand. He sat with her for several minutes. Then he stood up, and looked down at the body. A cold, intense anger, a feeling entirely foreign to him, welled up inside Billy as he visualized the brutal attack on a defenceless woman. Abruptly, he turned, and went out to saddle his horse.

Matt Hart, county sheriff, was sitting in his armchair on the sidewalk outside his office in Larraby when Billy rode into town and approached him.

'Howdy, Billy,' said the sheriff. 'Haven't seen your mother for quite a spell. She keeping well, Billy?'

Billy tied his horse to the hitching-rail.

'My mother's dead, Mr Hart,' he said. 'She's been murdered.'

The sheriffs eyes widened, and he eased his ponderous bulk from the armchair.

'You sure of that, Billy?' he asked. 'What happened?'

'She's dead, Mr Hart,' replied Billy. 'She was beaten up and strangled by somebody, and some money's been taken. I don't know who did it. I found her when I got back from town.'

The sheriff turned, and went into his office. Billy followed him.

'I'll go back with you right now, Billy,' he said. 'We ain't had anything like this happen before, leastwise not since I've been sheriff.'

'Before we go, Mr Hart,' said Billy, 'I have to do a couple of things. First I have to ask Mr Osborne to go out for my mother, and get her buried right. Then I have to find Seth Parker, and ask him to come back with us.'

'All right, Billy,' agreed the sheriff, 'but what do you want Seth for?'

'Well, Mr Hart,' answered Billy, 'Seth was a good friend of my father, and I heard him many a time yarning with my father about the days when he was an army scout, and I once heard the blacksmith say that Seth was one of the best trackers in the business.'

'All right, Billy,' said the sheriff. 'I figure I can read sign as good as most, but I've got to agree that Seth is in a class of his own. If that's the way you want it, ask him along.'

'Thank you, Mr Hart,' said Billy.

While the sheriff went to find his deputy, to instruct him to organize a posse, Billy went along to the small shack on the edge of town which was Seth Parker's home. Seth was a grizzled veteran in his late sixties.

'I guess you know, Billy, how sorry I am about your ma,' he said, on hearing the news of Mary's death.

'I know,' said Billy. 'You've been a good friend to us all.'

'You've no idea at all who did it?' asked Seth.

'No,' replied Billy, 'but I'm sure there was more than one. I swept the ground outside the house this morning, and when I got back it looked like there had been more than one horse there. They must have done it for the money. They emptied a cash-box that was under the floorboards. It had a lot of money in it, and a silver watch with a picture of ma in it, which belonged to my pa.'

'Like you said, Billy, they were probably after the money,' opined Seth. 'But why did they have to kill your ma as well?'

'That I don't know,' answered Billy. 'I came to ask you,' he went on, 'if you'd ride out with me and the sheriff so that you could look at the sign before it's all messed up. I want to know everything you can tell me about the men who did this. I figured you could do a better job of this than the sheriff.'

'Maybe so,' said Seth. 'I'll do the best I can, Billy, and give you and the sheriff all the information I can get.'

They joined the sheriff, who was waiting outside his office, and all three headed for the homestead. When they reached it, Seth went ahead, and closely inspected all the recent tracks in the vicinity of the house. Then he entered the house, to emerge several minutes later and motion the sheriff and Billy inside. The sheriff entered first, and walked to the bedroom. Billy followed him. The sheriff looked down at Mary Dare. His face hardened.

'Cold-blooded murderers!' he exclaimed.

'I've seen a few killings in my time, but nothing like this before. Well, Seth,' he went on, 'what do you make of those tracks?'

'There were three of them,' answered Seth. 'One was a big man on a big horse. The other two were probably about average size. One of these was dragging his left foot a mite, like he was lame. They all got off their horses, and went into the house. They rode in from the east, and when they left they headed west. One of the horses was a grey. You can see the tracks of the horses for yourselves. There's nothing special about the shoes.'

'That bandanna,' asked the sheriff. 'You seen that before, Billy?'

'It's mine,' replied Billy. 'Sometimes ma used it to cover her head.'

The sheriff got on his horse.

'I'm going back to town,' he announced. 'I'll get the posse on the move pronto. We'll get those killers, Billy.'

'I'm going with you,' said Billy.

'I can't take you,' said the sheriff. 'How

often have you handled a sidearm or a rifle, Billy?'

'I ain't handled a sidearm, but I used to go out with pa shooting rabbit with a rifle,' pleaded Billy.

'These men we're after,' said the sheriff grimly, 'they're killers, Billy, and every man in my posse has got to be used to handling a gun and a rifle. I've got to go now. We've got to get after those three while the trail is still fresh.'

The sheriff rode off in the direction of Larraby. Billy watched him go, then turned to Seth.

'Mr Parker,' he asked. 'I'd be obliged if you'd show me all that sign you saw around, so I can get it fixed in my mind.'

During the next half-hour they followed the tracks from the point, a quarter of a mile from the house, where the three men had briefly stopped, to the point outside the house where all three had dismounted. The tracks led in and out of the house, then off the property. Seth pointed out to Billy the scuffing mark made by the left boot of one of the men.

The funeral of Mary Dare took place two days later at the cemetery on the outskirts of Larraby. The Dares were a well-respected family, and there was a good attendance. Billy acknowledged the murmured condolences of the people present. As the coffin was lowered into the pit, next to the grave of Ben Dare, the terrible sense of loss hit him once again.

After the funeral, he made his way over to the sheriff's office, where he found one of the deputies, Phil Hurn, seated at the desk.

'Any news from the sheriff yet, Mr Hurn?' he asked.

'A homesteader came in about half an hour ago,' replied the deputy. 'He has a place west of here. He said the posse stopped at his place yesterday, and the sheriff said he was following a clear trail left by those killers. He reckoned they were less than a day behind them. We'll see them hang, Billy.' He paused. 'I sure was sorry about your mother,' he went on.

'Thanks,' said Billy.

He went along to Seth Parker's shack with the news, and the old man offered to let him know when the sheriff returned.

It was several days later when Seth rode up to the homestead. Billy was splitting logs behind the house. Seth dismounted stiffly, and walked over to him.

'The posse's back, Billy,' he said. 'Came in this morning. I've had a word with the sheriff. Seems they followed the trail to a town called Little Bluff. After that it just vanished. They scouted around for a while, but couldn't pick it up again, so they came back. The sheriff's sending out information about those three to any peace officers who might be likely to see them. He got a description of them from a bartender in Little Bluff. The bartender said there had been three strangers in the saloon. There was one big man and two smaller ones. The big man was around six foot two, running to fat, with a black beard, and real mean-looking. The bartender heard one of the other two men call him Arnie. The other two men were medium height, and slim built. One of them was dragging

21

his left foot like he had an old gunshot wound. The bartender said all three were wearing a gun tied low down, and looked like they knew how to use them. In fact, he said it was the meanest looking trio he'd had in there for a long time.'

'Does the sheriff have any "wanted" notices on those three?'

'He says not,' answered Seth.

'Well,' said Billy, 'now the sheriff hasn't been able to catch them, I'll have to go after them myself.'

Seth's jaw dropped.

'Goldarn it, Billy!' he protested. 'You're only eighteen! You wouldn't stand a chance against those three. They're murderers, and maybe professional gunfighters. Even if you only came up against one of them, you'd be as good as dead.'

'I wasn't figuring on taking off after them right away,' said Billy. 'First off, I've got to learn something about tracking, and how to handle a gun. I'd sure appreciate you giving me a few lessons on reading sign.'

'My eyes ain't quite what they used to

be when I was scouting for the army, Billy,' said Seth, 'but if you're really set on it, I guess I can show you a few things that might come in useful. I'd be glad to do it. Your ma and pa were the best friends I had around here.'

'Thanks,' said Billy. 'Now the other thing I want to ask you about is whether you know anybody around here who could teach me how to handle a sidearm well enough to give me a chance against those killers?'

'The more I think about it, Billy,' said Seth, 'the more I feel that it's not a good idea for you to chase after those three.'

'Let's look at it this way,' said Billy. 'Suppose *your* ma had been murdered when you were my age. Would *you* have been happy if the killers were riding around free, and you weren't doing anything about it?'

'Darn it! I've got to say no,' admitted Seth.

He looked hard at Billy. He saw a fair-haired, blue-eyed, good-looking youth of about five feet ten, with a compact body, well-muscled and tanned from his labours on the homestead. There was a set to his jaw that indicated his determination to hunt down the murderers. Seth decided that it would be fruitless to try to persuade him otherwise.

'It so happens,' he told Billy, 'that there's an old sidekick of mine living outside of Toshack—that's about a hundred miles west of here—who was reckoned, in his heyday, to be one of the slickest men with a handgun in Texas. And what's more, he was no slouch with a rifle either. His name is Jim Walsh. He was a lawman for about ten years. Maybe you've heard of him?'

'Yes,' replied Billy. 'I heard the black-smith talking about him one day, and he was saying that when you and Jim used to ride together, it was the toughest combination around at the time.'

'He was sure as hell right,' chuckled Seth, with a gleam in his rheumy eye. 'I could tell you some stories of those days that would make your hair curl, boy. Anyhow,' he went on, 'Jim and me were pretty close. I'll give you a letter for him, and ask him if he can help you. But I tell you, Billy, if Jim says you ain't got the makings of a natural gunfighter, then you'd better drop the idea of trailing those killers, because you wouldn't stand a chance in hell of nailing them. And another thing,' he went on, 'don't you buy any shooting-irons until you've seen Jim. He'll tell you what to get.'

'All right,' agreed Billy. 'And thanks.'

The next morning Billy spent a few hours at the homestead, attending to all the necessary chores. Then, around noon, he rode over to Seth's place for his first training session with the old scout, in the art of tracking.

'You've got to get this fixed in your head from the start, Billy,' explained Seth. 'The way most folks moves around, they might just as well have their eyes and ears closed for all the sign they picks up. A good tracker sees and hears and smells everything around him, and he can shut out the things that ain't important, and just concentrate on reading sign. And he trains himself so that all this comes natural-like. I reckon,' he went on, 'that the best trackers of all are the Indians. And the best Indian scouts I ever met up with myself were the Apache scouts I once worked with in Arizona.'

One of the trails into town passed close by Seth's place, and the two rode out along this, occasionally dismounting to allow Seth to point out various features of the tracks, such as the small difference in shoe-prints which distinguished one horse from another. Back in town, they sat on the sidewalk outside the saloon, while Seth indicated the footmarks made by riders who had dismounted at the hitching-rail. He surprised Billy by naming riders who had produced some of the prints.

'It's like I said, Billy,' remarked Seth. 'I sit here quite a lot, and without thinking about it, I notice the tracks made by the fellers who ride up here. You still remember those tracks we saw at your place, Billy?'

Billy's young face hardened.

'I ain't ever going to forget those,' he replied.

26

The sheriff, walking out of the hotel and making for his office, spotted the two, and came over to them.

'Hi, Seth. Hi, Billy,' he called. 'Sorry we didn't catch up with those killers, Billy. You understand I couldn't keep after them any longer when I figured they'd left my territory. I'm hoping they'll be picked up by another law officer when those wanted posters get around. What sort of plans have you got for the future, Billy?'

'First thing I've got to do,' answered Billy, 'is to sell up the homestead. I'll see if Mr Darvel at the bank knows anybody who might be interested. Then I can start getting ready to go after those three.'

The sheriff stared at Billy for a moment. Then he exploded.

'You're crazy!' he shouted. 'The law will take care of those killers. You ain't got a chance against them on your own.'

'I know you've done your best, Mr Hart,' said Billy, 'and I'm grateful, but the idea of those three riding free just doesn't seem right to me. I know you can't follow them, but *I* can. Just as soon as I'm ready, that is.'

The sheriff looked at Seth.

'He's set on it, sheriff,' said Seth.

'I'm giving you a final warning, Billy Dare,' said the sheriff sternly. 'You can't take the law into your own hands.'

Billy looked the sheriff in the eye. He said nothing. The sheriff shook his head angrily, and cursed. He turned, and walked off towards his office.

'How are you fixed for money, Billy?' enquired Seth.

'All our savings were stolen,' answered Billy, 'but when I sell the place, I should get enough to buy me a good horse and saddle, and anything else I need to start me off. And there'll be enough left to keep me on the trail for as long as it takes.'

The next morning Billy went to see the banker, Darvel, and explained his wish to sell the homestead. After expressing his condolences over the death of Billy's mother, the banker said he could think of two possible buyers, both of whom he would probably see during the coming week or two. He said he would let Billy know if either of them was interested.

While waiting for word from the banker, Billy resumed his sessions with Seth, during which they now roamed further afield, to give Seth an opportunity to show Billy how easy it was to lose a trail if ground conditions were not favourable, and what was the best way of finding it again. He also showed Billy how the dryness of horse-dung could be an indication of the length of time it had lain there, and how the warmth of the earth under the ashes of a dead fire could give an idea of how long ago it had been put out.

It was ten days after his visit to Darvel when the banker sent word for Billy to go and see him. He told Billy that he had a buyer for the homestead who was offering what was, in his opinion, a fair price, and he recommended that Billy should accept the offer. Billy agreed, and the banker said he would have the papers ready to sign in a couple of days. Billy went over to give Seth the news.

'When are you aiming to leave, Billy?' asked Seth. 'I've got to say that you've got a good eye for tracking, but it ain't possible to make a first-rate tracker in a few weeks. In fact, the best trackers are the ones who've spent a few years in the business. Howsomever, if we took another couple of weeks at it, I guess you'd be a lot better at tracking than most folks around here.'

'Right,' agreed Billy. 'Two more weeks. And I'd be obliged if you'd help me to find a good horse before I go.'

'So happens there's a horse for sale down at the livery stable,' Seth told him. 'What you want is a strong horse, and a fast one, and the bay gelding I've seen down there looks like it fits those requirements exactly. We'll go along and see it when you get your money. And take my advice, Billy, when you do get a good horse, treat it like a friend, and not like a cowpony is usually treated. That's the only way to get the best out of it. Don't forget that one day your life might depend on it.'

2

Two weeks later, Billy was ready to leave. He rode over to Seth's shack, dismounted from the bay gelding, and went over to shake the old man's hand.

'You take care, Billy,' said the old man. 'I'm going to miss those little jaunts we've been having lately. Give my regards to Jim Walsh, and take good heed of what he says. If anybody can make a gunfighter out of you, it's Jim. So long, boy.'

'So long, Mr Parker,' said Billy. 'I sure am obliged to you for all you've done. When I've finished this job, I'll come back and have a yarn with you about it.'

'You do that, Billy,' said Seth.

Billy rode up to the cemetery, and walked over to the graves of Ben and Mary Dare. He stood for a long time, motionless, with head bowed, looking back over the years, and thinking of his father and mother. Then he mounted the bay, and headed west.

Two days later, Billy rode into Little Bluff's one and only street, and tied up his horse outside the saloon. He went inside. The place was deserted, except for the bartender, a short, swarthy man with a long, drooping moustache and a lugubrious countenance. He eyed Billy as he approached the bar. He idly wondered who this fresh-faced youngster was, and what was his business in Little Bluff.

'Howdy,' he said.

'Howdy,' said Billy.

'Just passing through?' asked the bartender.

'Yes,' replied Billy, 'after I've got some information. I'd be obliged if you could help me.'

'Depends what you want to know,' said the bartender.

'A few weeks ago,' said Billy, 'you had three men in here that Sheriff Hart from Larraby was chasing. One of them was a big man called Arnie. They got clear away from the sheriff, and I was wondering if you could recollect anything about them that you didn't mention to Sheriff Hart which would maybe help me to find them.'

The bartender swatted a fly on top of the bar, and wiped off the remains with his bar-cloth.

'I can see you ain't the law,' he observed, 'so I'm a mite curious to hear why you want to find those three.'

'So happens they murdered my mother,' said Billy, quietly.

The bartender studied him closely. His first impulse was to advise the youthful stranger that, in his opinion, it would mean certain death for him to try and hunt down those three tough-looking desperadoes on his own. But there was a look in Billy's eye which warned him he would be wasting his breath. And, after all, it was none of his business.

'You want a drink?' he asked.

'Water, please, if you've got any,' replied Billy.

The bartender filled his glass with a muddy-looking liquid which Billy eyed with some distaste.

'Now let me think,' said the bartender. He closed his eyes, and a look of intense concentration furrowed his brow. After a short period, he opened his eyes again.

'There's just one thing,' he said. 'I didn't know about it until after the sheriff had gone. The stable-owner's boy was up in the loft at the livery stable, and he heard the big man speaking to one of the others when they came to pick up their horses. He only heard a piece of the conversation, but it was something about meeting up with somebody in Ellsworth, Kansas, around August. Can't think of anything else that would help.'

'Thanks,' said Billy. 'That helps a lot. It gives me something to go on.'

The next morning he left the rooming-house where he had spent the night, picked up his horse from the livery stable, and went over to the store for some provisions. Then he headed for Toshack, and the old gunfighter Jim Walsh.

Jim Walsh, seated on a bench just outside his log cabin located on a hillside ten miles north of Toshack, looked down into and along the valley below. The sun, low in the western sky, illuminated the valley floor and the solitary rider making his way up towards the cabin. Walsh went into the cabin, came out with a Winchester rifle, resumed his seat, and laid the rifle across his knees. Fifteen minutes later, Billy rode slowly up the last stretch of rough track leading to the cabin, and stopped in front of Walsh. He saw a tall, lean man, with sparse, grey hair, a neatly trimmed moustache, and, despite his age, a keen and piercing eye which was aimed in Billy's direction.

'Howdy,' said Billy. 'You Mr Walsh?'

'Yup,' replied Walsh.

'I'm Billy Dare,' said Billy. 'I've got a letter for you from Seth Parker over in Larraby.'

'That so?' said Walsh. 'Hand it over.'

Billy dismounted, and handed the letter to Walsh. Walsh opened the envelope, his eyes still on Billy. Then he laboriously read the letter. When he had finished reading, he looked up at Billy, and studied him for a while. Billy shifted his feet uneasily under the keen scrutiny, but he looked the old man in the eye until the latter spoke.

'How old are you, son?' he asked.

'Just turned eighteen,' replied Billy.

'And what makes you figure,' asked Walsh, 'that you've got the makings of a gunfighter?'

'I don't know whether I've got the makings of a gunfighter or not,' replied Billy, 'not having used a sidearm before. But I know that the more I get used to handling a gun, the easier it will be for me to hunt down the men who killed my mother. And that's what I'm aiming to do.'

'Seth Parker was a partner of mine for a long time,' said Walsh, 'and they don't come any better. He says you're set on hunting down those three men, and he asks me to give you as much help as I can. What I'm going to do first is to spend a few days finding out whether you've got any talent at all as a gunfighter. If you have, then we'll carry on from there. But I'm warning you,' he went on, 'that it's something you've really got to work hard at, and even if you do get to be good at it, you've still got to practise all the time.'

He rose from the bench.

'I've got some stew on the stove,' he said. 'Let's eat.'

The next morning after breakfast, Walsh and Billy went outside and sat on the bench together. Walsh had a revolver in his hand.

'This is a Colt Peacemaker .45, single action,' he told Billy. 'It ain't the gun I used to carry when I was in my prime, because it ain't been out all that long. But it's the best gun I ever handled up to now.'

He showed Billy how to load the gun, how to cock it by using the thumb joint over the hammer, and how to fire it.

'You can see this gun has chambers for six cartridges,' Walsh pointed out, 'but a top gunfighter would only load five, and he would leave the hammer on the empty chamber. That way, there is no danger of the gun going off in the holster.'

Walsh then took the gun to pieces, and

showed Billy how to clean and oil it, and then reassemble it.

'Do this regular,' he told Billy, 'and the gun won't let you down. And practise so that you can do it just as fast in the dark as in the daylight.'

During the rest of the time available that day, Billy took down and reassembled the gun a number of times and, with the chambers empty, he accustomed himself to the feel and balance of the gun, and the action of the cocking and firing mechanisms. The following morning, after he had helped Walsh with a few chores around the cabin, the two of them sat out on the bench again.

'The next thing we've got to think about,' said Walsh, 'is how to get the gun out of the holster, cock it, and fire it in exactly the right direction before the feller you're up against has gunned you down. You've got to realize that it's not much good getting a shot off in record time if it misses the target. Better to take just a little extra time, and get in an accurate shot.'

'What about fanning and hip-shooting?' asked Billy. 'I once heard the blacksmith in Larraby saying that some of the best gunfighters handled their guns that way.'

'That blacksmith was dead wrong,' said Walsh, 'and there's a crowd of fanners and hip-shooters on Boot Hill to prove it. The best gunfighters take their time, and hit the target first go. What you've got to do now,' he went on, 'is to practise getting the gun out of the holster. We'll deal with the cocking and firing later.'

He went into the cabin, and came out wearing a gunbelt and a holstered gun. He stood in front of Billy.

'Watch,' he said.

In one swift movement, his wrist bent downward, his hand grasped the handle of the gun, and he drew it smoothly upward until the end of the barrel just cleared the holster. At this exact moment he raised the end of the barrel to a level position, and at the same time moved the gun slightly forward, and into a position just above waist level. He repeated the movement in slow-motion a dozen times, then took off the gunbelt and fastened it round Billy's waist.

'Now, for the rest of today, and tomorrow,' he instructed, 'practise pulling that gun out of the holster and levelling it like I showed you. If you feel that the holster wants to be lower or higher, move it to the position that suits you best.'

Two days later Walsh demonstrated to Billy the complete action of drawing, cocking, pointing and triggering the gun in one smooth-flowing movement. Billy practised this movement, with Walsh's help, over the next few days, and he gradually achieved a smooth drawing and firing action. The handle of the gun fitted snugly into his right hand, and he was getting the reassuring feeling that the gun was part of him.

'Not bad,' said Walsh approvingly, a week to the day after Billy had arrived. 'Your draw is smooth enough, but you've got to keep practising to work up some more speed. In a few days we'll start using a loaded gun, and see how good you are at hitting a target.

'Maybe you've been wondering,' he added, 'whether it's a good idea to wear two guns. A lot of gunfighters, including peace officers, do this, because two guns can be useful if one man is facing a crowd. In your case, you've just got one natural gun-hand, and I reckon we'd better concentrate on that one. If you want to wear another gun later on, that's up to you.'

A few days later, when Walsh was satisfied that Billy's speed on the draw was improving, he produced a target board, about six feet by two feet, which he had constructed from some old planks, and he fixed this to two posts set in the ground, with the six-foot sides vertical. He took Billy over to a position about sixteen yards from the board, and handed him a box of cartridges.

'If you're in a gunfight and you hit a man at sixteen yards, you're doing pretty good,' he told Billy. 'That's why I'm standing you here. What I want you to do is to practise firing single shots at that target board until you're pretty sure where the bullet is going to hit. Take it slow and easy-like at first, and gradually work up speed as you go along. So far, you're handling the gun fine. What you've got to go after now is speed and accuracy.

'I'm going into Toshack for a couple of days,' he went on, 'to see an old sidekick of mine who lives there. I'll bring back some provisions, and some more ammunition. There are plenty more cartridges in the cabin for you to be going on with.'

Walsh returned a couple of days later, in mid-afternoon.

'Right,' he greeted Billy. 'Let's see how you're coming on.'

He tacked a piece of paper, about nine inches square, onto the target board, about four and a half feet from the ground.

'I want you to stand a bit closer this time,' he said. 'Here will do. Now I want you to draw as quick as you can, and fire a single shot at that paper.'

Billy did as requested, while Walsh closely observed the draw. Walsh then walked over to inspect the target. The bullet had hit at almost the exact centre of the paper.

'You had a bit of luck there, Billy,' he called. 'You hit the paper, and what's more you hit her plumb centre—or pretty near. Now, just to prove you ain't a second Wild Bill Hickock, just fire off the last four shots. Make a fresh draw for each shot.'

Billy complied, then he and Walsh walked up to the target together. Walsh's jaw dropped as he inspected it. All five bullet-holes were grouped closely around the centre of the target. For a long moment he looked at the holes. Then he turned to Billy.

'When you brought me that letter, Billy,' he said, 'I never figured that you might turn out to be a natural gunfighter. But now I'm beginning to wonder. You've only been here two weeks, but you've already worked up to a smooth, quick draw, and what's more, there ain't many men toting a six-gun who could put five bullets as close as you did.

'What you've got to do now,' he went on, 'is to keep on practising until you find out how quick you can draw and fire without losing accuracy. Then you've got to practise firing one shot after another, as quickly as you can, with the same accuracy. And you've got to remember that there'll be times when you or your target, or maybe both, will be moving, so you'll have to practise drawing and firing while you're on the move, and also while your target is moving. I'll rig up a moving target on a line for you to practise on.'

During the next six weeks, Billy practised assiduously under the watchful eye of Walsh. At the end of this time, his speed on the draw had improved substantially, and the accuracy of his shooting, and the cat-like agility he displayed while both he and his target were on the move, drew a grunt of approval from his teacher.

'I don't want you to get no swollen head, Billy,' he said, 'but I've got to tell you that you're better now than I ever was, even in my prime. I can't teach you any more. I reckon you're ready to take up the trail after those killers, if that's what you're still set on doing.'

'I am,' said Billy. 'I'll leave in the morning. I'll be heading for Ellsworth. The only thing I've got to go on is that they might be there later this year.'

'There's one last thing I've got to say about the teaching you've been getting here,' warned Walsh. 'All the time, you've been shooting at a target that can't shoot back. I can't say how you're going to measure up when you're up against somebody who's set on gunning you down. That's something you won't know until it happens. I'll be wishing you the best of luck.'

3

The next morning, as Billy was saddling his horse for his departure, Walsh came out of the cabin with the Colt Peacemaker and gunbelt which Billy had been using for the past eight weeks. He handed them to Billy.

'I'd like you to have these,' he said. 'It'll save you having to get used to a new gun, and I'll be glad if you can use it on them murderers. Danged if I wouldn't come with you if I was ten years younger. Let me know how you get on, won't you, boy?'

Billy thanked the old gunfighter, and promised to look him up when his mission was completed. Then he mounted the bay, and rode off down the valley towards Toshack, where he bought supplies, and ammunition for the Peacemaker, and for the Winchester rifle which had belonged

46

to his father. Walsh had tried out the rifle, and had given him a few pointers which had improved his accuracy. Having completed his purchases, Billy headed north.

The following day, about fifty miles north of Toshack, Lois Sinclair was out riding on the Circle T ranch, a spread owned by her husband Dan. They had moved out west twelve years earlier, and had built up a sizeable herd, and Dan was now one of the most respected and influential men in the area. Lois was an attractive, raven-haired woman of about forty, with a well-contoured figure. She was ten years younger than her husband. No child had arrived to bless the union, and this was a source of considerable sorrow and disappointment to them both. The time had long since gone when Lois had worked a long, hard day helping Dan to establish the ranch. Now, she had help in the ranch-house, and sometimes she found time hanging rather heavily on her hands. She was an accomplished horsewoman, and spent much of her free time riding around the range.

On this particular day she was riding her favourite horse through a small canyon about six miles north of the ranch-house, heading for a small lake, which was one of her favourite spots. She was just approaching a sharp bend in the canyon floor, when she heard two riders coming up from behind. Her first thought was that the riders were two of her husband's cowhands. Then, as they came abreast, she realized that she had never seen them before.

As the two men passed her, then swung round to block her path, she could see that one of their horses was limping badly. She was forced to come to a halt.

One of the men was short, fat and swarthy, with a severe cast in his right eye which gave him a particularly villainous-looking appearance. Even without this cast, he would still have been an ugly-looking character. The second man was tall and slim, with a long face, which wore what appeared to be a permanent sneer. Both men wore guns, and looked like they knew how to use them.

'Well, well!' exclaimed the fat man, closely eyeing Lois's mount. 'What have we here? It's just like the answer to a prayer, ain't it, Walt? Here we are, with a horse just about ready to drop, and a posse not that far behind, and a fine animal like this turns up, just asking for a good fast run.'

The thin man's sneer deepened a little.

'Sure is, Dave,' he replied. 'And nobody around here to interfere. Ain't seen man or cow for quite a spell.'

Lois started to wheel her horse, in a frantic effort to escape, but the thin man caught her bridle, grabbed the neck of her shirt, which tore as he pulled her towards him, and slapped her hard on the face. She cried out, and recoiled. Then she forced herself to speak calmly.

'My husband owns this ranch,' she said, 'and if you take my horse by force, he'll hunt you down and kill you both.'

Ignoring her, the two men dismounted, and stood in front of her mount.

It was at that moment that Billy Dare rode slowly around the bend, coming up behind the two men. The ground was soft, and the two men were concentrating their attention on Lois. They did not hear Billy approach. He observed the torn shirt, the hand on the bridle of the woman's horse, and the well-worn handles of the holstered guns carried by the two men. He also saw the look of despair on the woman's face, and he knew that the cry he had heard as he approached the bend had not been imagined.

As Billy continued towards them, the fat man was moving nearer Lois with the intention of pulling her down from her horse. As he reached for her, he turned slightly, and caught sight of Billy out of the corner of his eye.

'Walt!' he yelled.

As both men started to wheel round to face him, Billy erupted into action. Kicking his feet free of the stirrups, he fell sideways off his horse, hit the ground, and went into a roll, during which the Peacemaker spoke twice. The fat man was just about to trigger his gun when Billy's first shot hit him in the forehead. His partner's shot ploughed into the ground only inches to one side of Billy, just before Billy's second shot hit him in the chest. The fat man was dead before he hit the ground. The other man died seconds later.

Lois's mare, startled by the gunfire, reared, almost unseating her, then ran off. Billy mounted his own horse to chase after her. Then he saw that she was bringing the mare under control. She rode slowly back towards him, and stopped short of the two bodies lying on the ground. She was shaking a little, but she sat in silence for a few moments while Billy took a look at the two bodies, and soon brought herself under control. Then she spoke.

'Are they both dead?' she asked.

'I reckon so,' replied Billy.

'I'm Lois Sinclair,' she said. 'My husband Dan owns this ranch.'

'I'm pleased to meet you, ma'am,' said Billy. 'My name is Billy Dare.'

'Well, Billy Dare, I'm obliged to you,' said Lois. 'I certainly am glad you were riding this way today. It's a long time since we had scum like these two riding across our range. They have a lame horse, and they were just going to take mine when you showed up. When I saw you facing up to them, I figured you were as good as dead. I could hardly believe it when I saw those two go down.'

'I'm glad I happened along, ma'am,' said Billy. He looked down at the two bodies. He had no feeling of remorse. He was sure that if he hadn't out-gunned the two men, he himself would now be dead.

'I'm riding back to the ranch-house,' said Lois. 'Dan will get some of the hands to come out for these two. I'd like you to come with me, if you will.'

Billy agreed, and later, as they approached the ranch buildings, which lay in a shallow valley, he could see that it was a big spread. There was a large, two-storey dwelling-house, also a cookshack, bunkhouse, large corral and sheds. A small, winding stream ran close to the buildings.

There were two hands standing outside the bunkhouse. Lois, holding the torn front of her shirt together, stopped near them, and dismounted. Billy did the same. Lois spoke to the two men.

'This is a friend of mine, boys,' she said. 'His name is Billy Dare. Is my husband back yet?'

'He's in the house,' replied one of the men.

Lois turned to Billy.

'I'd like you to wait here while I see my husband. Will you do that, please?'

'Yes, ma'am,' replied Billy.

A few minutes later, as he was idly chatting with the two hands, the ranch-house door flew open, and a large figure erupted, and strode quickly towards him. Dan Sinclair was well over six feet, with reddish, thinning hair, piercing blue eyes, and a powerful frame. He came to a stop in front of Billy.

'Billy Dare,' he said. 'I've just heard what a good job you did out there. I'm going out for those two men now, but I'd sure like to see you when I get back. You go in the cookshack, and the cook'll fix up a meal for you.'

'Thank you, Mr Sinclair,' said Billy. 'I'll

be here when you get back.'

Dan turned to the two hands.

'Saddle up, boys,' he ordered. 'We've got a job to do.'

It was over an hour and a half before Dan Sinclair returned alone. He rode over to Billy, who was standing outside the bunkhouse with one of the hands. He dismounted, and handed his horse to the ranch-hand. Then he spoke to Billy.

'The hands I took out with me are taking those two over to the sheriff in Grafton,' he explained. 'They sure is a mean-looking pair. My guess is that Sheriff Carter has "wanted" posters on those two. My wife can tell him what happened, but I guess he'll be wanting a word with you as well.' He turned towards the house. 'Come on inside,' he invited.

Billy followed Dan into the house. The interior was comfortably furnished, and numerous signs of a woman's touch were in evidence. Lois rose from her chair as they entered. She moved towards Billy, stood in front of him, and took his hands in hers. She looked him straight in the eye.

'Billy Dare,' she said. 'I'm only going to say this once, because I've got a feeling you'll find it embarrassing. If you hadn't happened along, those two men would have taken my horse, and maybe roughed me up a bit more as well. A boy like you standing up to those two was one of the bravest things I've seen, and I thank God you came to no harm.'

Billy flushed with acute embarrassment. Before he could think of anything to say in reply, Dan spoke.

'That's the way I feel too, Billy,' he said. 'I had a look at the sign back there, and that sure was a neat piece of gunplay on your part. What I can't figure out is why, when you've got such an educated gun-hand as that, I ain't heard the name of Billy Dare before?'

'The reason is simple,' explained Billy. 'I ain't ever shot anybody before. In fact, up to a few months ago, I was running a little homestead near Larraby with my mother, and I'd never had a six-shooter in my hand.' He went on to tell them of the events that had followed since then.

As he finished, there was silence for a few moments. Then Lois spoke.

'I'm so very sorry, Billy,' she said. 'I guess you miss your mother an awful lot. Maybe you'd like to stay with us awhile before you start out on the trail again. And maybe my husband can give you some ideas about how to find those three.'

'I figure you've thought pretty hard about what you're taking on, Billy,' said Dan, 'so I guess there's no use trying to change your mind. You say there's a chance they may be in Ellsworth in August?'

'Yes,' replied Billy. 'It's the only thing I've got to go on up to now.'

'Then I've got an idea,' said Dan. 'Right now, we're rounding up a herd of about 2,500 head for a trail-drive up to Ellsworth, starting day after tomorrow. Maybe you'd like to go along. The trail boss is John Ward. He's a good friend of mine, and I know he needs an extra hand. And maybe the money will come in handy. And you'd be in Ellsworth well before August.'

'I ain't ever been on a round-up or a trail-drive before, Mr Sinclair,' Billy pointed out, 'but I'd like to go along if Mr Ward will have me.'

'It'll be all right, Billy,' Dan reassured him. 'John Ward has a good bunch of hands, and they'll soon lick you into shape. Maybe you'll have to stand a bit of joshing, but there'll be nothing mean about it. I'll take you out to the herd tomorrow.

'And there's one other thing,' he went on. 'I've got a good friend in Ellsworth. He had a small spread near here, and I did him a good turn or two, but his wife hankered after town life, so he sold out, and started up a livery stable and store in Ellsworth. I hear he's doing fine. I'll give you a letter for him. Maybe he'll be able to help you in some way. His name is Butler, Mark Butler.'

The following morning, Billy, sitting outside the bunkhouse, saw the sheriff ride up to the ranch-house, dismount, and go inside. Some time later, he came out with Dan Sinclair, who called Billy over. The sheriff eyed Billy curiously as he approached.

'This is Sheriff Carter, Billy,' said Dan. 'He'd like you to tell him just what happened out there yesterday.'

After Billy had described his encounter with the two men, the sheriff spoke.

'From what Mrs Sinclair and you have told me,' he said, 'it seems that those two got just what they deserved. In any case, they were both wanted men on the run, and due for hanging. The fat man was Dave Connors, and the other was Walt Manley. They're both wanted for bank robbery and murder. One of the people they murdered was a woman. Manley had a reputation as one of the deadliest gunslingers around, and Connors was no slouch with a gun either.

'It seems to me,' the sheriff went on, looking hard at Billy, 'that you've got a special talent for gunplay, and you've got to be careful that killing doesn't get to be a habit. There've been too many young gunfighters who ended up as killers on the wrong side of the law.'

'I don't aim to end up like that, Mr Carter,' said Billy. 'But there's one thing I've got to do.'

'Yeah,' said the sheriff, testily. 'Mr Sinclair told me. But take good heed of what I said.'

4

The following morning, Billy rode out with Dan Sinclair to the herd. Lois had bidden him farewell, and had made him promise to let them know how his mission progressed. John Ward, the trail boss, saw them coming, and rode out to meet them. He was a thickset, middle-aged man of medium height, a former army scout, who had been trail-driving for the past eight years. He had a reputation for being tough, but fair, with his trail-hands. Also, he had a reputation for delivering a herd more or less on time, with a minimum loss of cattle. His services were in much demand.

After a private conversation between Sinclair and Ward, the two men rode over to Billy. Ward looked him over.

'I'm putting you on trial for a few days,' he told Billy. 'If I see you've got the makings of a good trail-hand, you're hired. Thirty a month and found.'

'Thank you, Mr Ward,' said Billy. 'I'll do the best I can.'

'I've got a cook and a wrangler, and seven cowhands, including yourself,' the trail boss told Billy, 'and the drive starts tomorrow at dawn.'

He pointed to a man sitting near the chuckwagon.

'That's Hank Rivers,' he said. 'Hank's a top cowhand. He's been on more trail-drives than he can remember. And he's never let me down. You go and have a yarn with him. He'll tell you what work you'll have to do, and he'll tell you how to do it. And mind you take good heed of what he says.'

Billy took his leave of Dan Sinclair, promising to keep in touch, and walked his horse across to the small temporary corral not far from the chuckwagon. Then he walked over to Hank. Hank was a small, wiry man, with a weatherbeaten face, a drooping moustache, and a humorous expression. Billy liked the look of him.

He looked up as Billy approached.

'My name is Billy Dare,' said Billy. 'Mr Ward took me on for a few days on trial. He told me you would tell me about the work I have to do. I've never been on a round-up or a trail-drive before.'

Hank looked at him pityingly.

'You all right in the head, son?' he queried. 'I only asked,' he went on, before Billy could reply, 'because no sane man who had any option would take on a trail-hand's job. A trail-hand is lucky if he gets four hours' sleep a day. Half of the rest of his time is spent either running in front of a stampeding herd, getting half-drowned on a river-crossing, or providing target practice for Indians. Whichever way you look at it, it's a mighty hard way to earn thirty dollars a month.'

'Mr Ward said you'd been a trail-hand for a long time,' ventured Billy.

'True,' said Hank, 'but when I first started, I was young and foolish like you. Now I've got some sense, it's too late to change. Howsomever,' he went on, 'if you're set on coming along, I can let you know exactly what you're in for.'

'I'd be obliged,' said Billy.

'Right,' said Hank. 'First off, let me tell you that when the trail boss tells you to do something, you do it right, and you do it pronto. If you don't do these two things, he has a way with words of telling you what he thinks of you that makes your hair curl. And if you make the same mistake twice, you're fired.

'Now next to the trail boss,' he went on, 'the most important man in the outfit is the cook, so you've got to stay in *his* favour. He's the boss around the chuckwagon. If you've got a good cook on the drive, then now and again, just for a few minutes, you might forget about them other bad things I mentioned. The cook's in town just now, but you'll see him later. He answers to the name of Henry Black, and he's famous for some of the meals he dishes up, particularly his red bean pie and sourdough biscuits. Another thing he does is to keep us headed in the right direction. Every night, he points the chuckwagon tongue to the North Star.

63

'As for the work,' went on Hank, 'it boils down to sitting on a horse for most of the time, and helping to get a herd from one place to another without losing too many head, and without the cows losing too much weight. You can lose cattle by drowning at river-crossings, in stampedes, or maybe to thieving Indians or rustlers. They can lose weight if water is scarce and grass is poor on the way. So the trail boss has to take these things into account when he's planning the drive. As for yourself, your best plan is to copy what the other trail-hands are doing when the drive starts tomorrow, and you'll soon get the hang of it.'

It was shortly after this conversation took place that the cook returned from town. He was a long-standing friend of Hank's, and after putting his horse in the corral, he walked over to him. He was a short, lean man of about sixty, with a completely bald head, but sporting a luxurious white beard.

'There's been a bit of excitement in town, Hank,' he said. 'Seems that a couple of days ago Dan Sinclair's wife was out riding on the range when two fellers stopped her, and started to rough her up. They wanted her horse, on account of one of theirs was lame. According to the sheriff, they were a couple of wanted men, Dave Connors and Walt Manley. They both had reputations as gunslingers, and both were wanted for murder.'

'I've heard of those two,' said Hank, 'and nothing good either.'

'Well,' Black went on, 'just as one of them was going to pull Mrs Sinclair off her horse, a young feller rode round a bend in the canyon towards them. Sheriff says he can't be more than seventeen or eighteen years old. He sized the situation up pretty quick, and took a roll off his horse, and plugged those two in the middle of it. One of them didn't even get a shot off. The other one did, but missed. They're both dead.'

'Some shooting,' commented Hank.

'Sure was,' agreed Black, 'especially for a feller who'd never pulled a gun on a man before—so the sheriff said.'

'What was this young feller's name?' asked Hank, curiously.

'It was Billy Dare,' replied Black.

'I figured it might be,' said Hank. 'And now I've got some news for you, Henry. When suppertime comes around, young Billy Dare will be eating whatever fancy concoction you've got lined up for us this evening. He came along with Dan Sinclair a while ago, and Mr Ward took him on. You can see him over there, talking to the wrangler.'

The cook looked in Billy's direction, and studied him for a few moments.

'Well, I'm danged!' he said. 'He sure don't look like no gunfighter to me. It's hard to believe that a youngster like that could get the better of Connors and Manley.'

'Sure is,' agreed Hank.

They watched Billy for a while, then Hank spoke.

'Have any of the other hands been in town today, Dare Henry?' he asked.

'Not that I know of,' replied Black.

'So the only ones on the drive that know

about Billy Dare's gunplay are you and me, and probably the trail boss?' said Hank.

'I guess so,' agreed Black.

'Right,' said Hank, 'then how about us keeping it that way if we can. We'd just be starting up a load of trouble for Billy Dare if we passed the word around about the shooting. You know what happens when a young feller gets a reputation as a gunfighter. He's certain to meet up with a few gunslingers who figure they're better than he is, and are looking to build up their reputations. And I reckon he'll get on better with the other trail-hands if they know nothing about this business.'

'You're dead right,' agreed Black, 'but you'd better tell Mr Ward how we aim to play this.'

Hank walked over to the trail boss, and discussed the matter with him. Ward agreed that the rest of the crew should be kept ignorant of Billy's part in the recent gunfight.

At first light the following morning the cook called the hands to breakfast. After eating this, they threw their bedrolls onto the chuckwagon, took a horse from the remuda, rode out to the herd, and began to put the cattle on the trail. The trail-drive had begun. The trail-hands gradually shaped the herd into a narrow column, heading in the direction picked out by the trail boss. Billy was placed in the drag position, at the rear of the herd. He could see that this would not be a popular position, since, in addition to enduring the discomfort of riding through the dust kicked up by the herd, the drag-riders had the job of harassing any slower moving cattle to make them keep up with the rest of the herd. However, Billy learned from his fellow drag-rider Jud Knowles, that the trail-hands took turns at riding in this position.

When he sat down for supper on that first day of the drive, Billy was saddle-sore and weary. However, he was learning fast, and he figured that, in a few days, he would be able to do his share of the work just as well as the rest.

The drive went well for the first week.

Good grazing and water were plentiful, and the weather was good. Billy chatted with Hank whenever he got the chance. Hank told him of his experiences over the years on previous drives, and also with the Pony Express. Billy was particularly enthralled by Hank's account of his time with the latter.

'I was a Pony Express rider,' Hank told him proudly, while they were taking supper one evening, 'from the time the service started until the time it folded up—about a year and a half, I reckon. The full run was from Missouri to California, and took about ten days. We changed horses every twelve miles or so, and handed over to another rider after we'd tired out maybe six mounts.'

'I expect those riders were hand-picked,' suggested Billy.

'They sure were,' agreed Hank. 'Though I says it, it wasn't a job for a weakling. There were a few riders, including Bill Cody, who rode non-stop over three hundred miles in an emergency.'

'What horses did you ride?' asked Billy.

'Generally mustangs, strong and well broke, and grain fed,' replied Hank. 'You've got to remember that a lot of riders were liable to run up against hostile Indians, so their mounts had to be fast, as well as strong.'

As the friendship between the two ripened, the time came when Hank told Billy that he and the cook knew of his encounter with Connors and Manley, but that they had decided not to tell the other hands about it. Billy was grateful. He told Hank about his mother's death, and his determination to find the men responsible.

'You picked yourself a tough job there, Billy,' commented Hank, 'and I sure hope you can carry it through, and come out in one piece.'

On the eighth night of the drive, the herd was bedded down near the small town of Burley, and it was there, early the following morning, that Billy experienced his first stampede.

Hank, on the first day of the drive, had already warned him of the dangers.

'Often,' he had said, 'you ain't got no idea they're about to take off, and there don't seem no reason for it at all. Other times, maybe a flash of lightning, or a roll of thunder, or some other noise will set them off. Sometimes they go the whole way without stampeding. Other times you get maybe three or four stampedes on a drive.

'If it does happen,' he had told Billy, 'follow me, and do the same as I do.'

It was just around dawn that it happened. Hank and Billy were on night guard. The night had been sultry, and the cattle nervous. There was tension in the air. Then a vivid flash of lightning, with an instantaneous crack of thunder, directly overhead, brought the cattle to their feet, and immediately they were off. Hank raced alongside the stampeding herd in an effort to get in front. Billy followed him. After three miles or so, they both got ahead sufficiently to allow them to rein back and slow down the herd. Then the other hands arrived on the flank, just behind the front of the stampede, and pressed in to turn the herd. Two of the punchers fired revolvers in the faces of the cattle, to accelerate the turn. The cattle began to circle, and eventually to mill.

The stampede was over.

The day following the stampede they reached Red River Station, a relatively easy fording-point on the Red River, the border between Texas and the Indian Territory. When they arrived, the river was fairly high, but the trail boss judged that it was still safe to cross. He decided to take the herd over immediately, to avoid the risk of any further rise in water-level. He gave the order to move the herd into the water.

The hands took up similar positions as on land, and eased the herd into the river. When it became too deep for the herd to walk, they swam, with the cowponies following suit. Billy, a good swimmer, felt no concern for his own safety, but he knew from the talk around the camp-fire the previous evening that most of the hands didn't relish the prospect of a deep-water crossing, and were mighty relieved when they reached the far bank. This particular crossing was completed without incident, and the herd was bedded down for the night in the Indian Territory.

Billy had already heard from Hank of the perils of crossing the Indian Territory. According to Hank, there were three things that the Indians coveted most—cattle, horses and money—and when a trail-drive, which could provide all three items, crossed their territory, the temptation to help themselves was, in some cases, too hard to resist. On some occasions, Hank told Billy, the Indians would simply start a stampede, and drive off some cattle in the confusion, without attacking the camp. On others, they would attack the camp, maybe killing or wounding some of the herders, and would stampede the cattle, and make off with horses, cattle and anything else they could lay their hands on. Hank did say, however, that the last trail-drive he had been on through the Indian Territory had been mostly trouble free, and he thought that maybe things were quietening down. He thought this was probably because most trail bosses now bought off trouble by giving the Indians a few cattle.

The trail boss summed up the situation to the hands that evening.

'I'm hoping we won't run into any trouble passing through the Indian Territory,' he said, 'but there's always a chance that we'll meet up with a bunch of young braves running wild. Most likely they'd be Comanches, who ride all over the Indian Territory. So everybody keep his eyes and ears skinned. And wear your guns if you like, just so long as you don't shoot one another.'

For the next three days they saw no sign of Indians. Then the trail boss spotted a group in the distance. As he watched closely, the group rode slowly up, and halted ahead of the herd. One of the Indians approached the trail boss. He asked for beef. The trail boss agreed they could take one steer. This they did, and departed peacefully.

'Let's hope they don't bother us no worse than that,' said the trail boss, as the Indians rode off.

It was fifteen days into Indian Territory,

at the noon stop, when real trouble hit unexpectedly. Hank and Billy were out watching the herd, and the rest of the hands and the trail boss were eating. Suddenly, over the top of a rise about two hundred yards from the herd, and on the opposite side of the herd from the chuckwagon, a bunch of yelling Comanches, nine strong, galloped into view, heading straight for Billy and the herd, and firing off their rifles. Billy quickly dismounted, pulled his gun, and crouched down by the side of his horse. A bullet passed close to his ear, and a second one plucked the sleeve of his shirt. Then, just before the startled herd stampeded in earnest, he straightened up, and had time to loose off three shots at the Indians, who had slowed right down as they came up to the herd. Three of the Indians went down. Startled, the remaining six wheeled off sharply to one side, then wheeled back when they were out of range, and followed the stampeding herd, which was headed for the chuckwagon.

Hank, mounted, was on the other side of the herd from Billy, and he was almost immediately caught up in the stampede. His horse started to turn as the herd moved towards it, then stumbled, and went down. Hank was unseated, and disappeared beneath the pounding hooves. His horse rose again, and ran off with the herd. Billy saw Hank go down, and he mounted, and galloped after the herd to the spot where he had last seen his friend.

Meanwhile the trail boss, cook and hands had taken shelter from the stampede behind the chuckwagon, from which they hauled out a couple of rifles, and managed to hit one of the Indians who were following the herd. The injured brave slowed down for a moment, and reeled in his saddle. Then he straightened up, and with the rest he followed the rapidly-disappearing herd which, as it skirted the remuda, had stampeded the horses.

When Billy reached the spot where Hank had gone down, his worst fears were realized. He dismounted, and stared, horrified, at the shapeless bundle left by the stampeding herd. It was some time before he was able to pull himself together. When he did so, he reloaded his gun, and rode back to look at the three Indians lying on the ground. So far as he could tell, they were all dead. Their bodies were hidden from the men at the chuckwagon by a rise in the ground. He rode over to the chuckwagon, where the trail boss was shouting orders to the hands.

'Hank's done for, Mr Ward,' he said. 'He went down when the stampede started. He didn't stand a chance.'

'Damn those Indians!' exploded Ward. 'Hank was a first-class trail-hand, and I've known him a long time. But we can't tend to him now, Billy. The first thing we have to do is go after the herd. We'll see to Hank when we get back.'

He called one of the hands over.

'Take Billy's horse, Jud,' he ordered, 'and round up some horses for the hands pronto.

'I'm leaving you here with the cook, Billy,' he went on, 'just in case those thieving devils come back. Mind you keep a sharp lookout.'

When sufficient horses were rounded up,

the trail boss left two with Billy and the cook, then led his men on the trail of the herd. Billy watched them go. Then he turned to the cook.

'Mr Black,' he said, 'What should we do about those Indians I shot down?'

'What Indians?' asked the cook sharply.

'Well,' replied Billy, 'when those Indians charged the herd, I managed to get three shots off when they were pretty close up, and I dropped three of them. I had a look at them, and I figure they're dead.'

The cook looked at Billy with respect.

'Three shots and three dead Indians,' he commented. 'That's pretty classy shooting with a six-shooter, Billy, considering you had a crowd of those braves charging right at you. Let's go and take a look.'

They took the two horses left by Ward, and rode first to the place where Hank had fallen. They stopped their horses, and looked down at the mangled remains.

'What a way to die!' exclaimed the cook, shaken by the sight. 'I never figured Hank would end up like this. He and I go back a long ways. He was a good friend.'

They moved on towards the place where Billy had been when the stampede started. The cook could now see the three bodies sprawled on the ground. He dismounted.

'Cover me, Billy,' he said, 'just in case any of these braves ain't quite finished.'

Billy dismounted and drew his gun. Then he followed the cook as he walked from one body to another, examining each one in turn. Completing his task, the cook turned to Billy.

'I see you got them all in the head,' he observed, 'and they're all dead. It's up to the trail boss what we do with these bodies. I guess he'll just leave them here.'

They rode back to the chuckwagon, which had not itself been damaged by the stampede, and cleared up the area around it, which bore signs of the stampeding herd. Then the cook busied himself around the chuckwagon, while Billy kept his eyes skinned for approaching riders. It was nearing dusk when the trail boss and the wrangler rode up, leading horses for the chuckwagon.

'We've got the herd stopped about four miles north,' the trail boss told them. 'We'll bed them down there for the night. We'll see to Hank now, and then we'll go along to the herd. Come morning, we'll look for any strays that ain't been driven off by those Indians.'

Taking two shovels from the chuck-wagon, the four of them rode over to Hank's remains. Billy and the wrangler dug a suitable pit, and gently lowered the corpse into it. They filled the hole in, then all four stood silent for a moment, before mounting. As the trail boss turned his horse, and started off towards the chuckwagon, the cook called after him.

'We've got some dead Indians over there, Mr Ward,' he said, pointing.

The trail boss pulled up sharply.

'Dead Indians!' he exclaimed. 'How come?'

'Well,' explained the cook, 'Billy managed to get three shots off just before the stampede started, and he brought three of those braves down.'

The trail boss stared at Billy in the

gathering dusk. Then he turned to the cook.

'Show me,' he said. 'And you two go hitch up the chuckwagon,' he ordered Billy and the wrangler.

He followed the cook towards the bodies of the three Indians. He walked over to each one, and took a close look. When he got back to the chuckwagon, he stopped in front of Billy.

'Were you aiming for the head, Billy?' he asked curiously.

'Yes,' replied Billy. 'I was afoot at the time, so that I could get some steady shots in, and there wasn't much else I could aim at.'

'Now that I've seen those dead Indians,' said the trail boss, 'I've got a feeling that we won't be bothered again by that particular bunch. Not after they've lost three braves, and one injured, and we lost only one that maybe they don't know about anyway. Let's get back to the herd.'

Early next morning the search for strays began. When these had been rounded up, and brought back to the herd, the trail boss found he was fifteen head short.

'It could have been a lot worse,' said Ward, 'if none of those braves had been killed.'

When the drive started up again, Billy greatly missed Hank, who had been his only real friend in the outfit. The other hands, who had heard from the wrangler about Billy's shoot-out with the Indians, now treated him with some reserve. Although most of them owned a gun, it was more often than not left in a bedroll during a drive, and none of them could claim any real skill in the use of the weapon. So it seemed that Billy's expertise with the Peacemaker set him a little apart from themselves.

It was twelve days later when, without further incident, they drove the herd out of the Indian Territory, and headed north for Ellsworth, which they reached two weeks later, with the cows in good condition.

The trail boss stopped the herd a few miles out of town. Then he rode in alone to make a deal for the cattle. It was suppertime when he returned. He dismounted, and walked over to the eating hands.

'We've got a buyer for the herd, men,' he announced. 'We hand it over at the stock-pens tomorrow.'

After the herd had been handed over the following day, Ward paid off the men.

5

Billy took his leave of the trail boss, mounted his own horse, which he had brought along on the drive, and rode into town. Like most of the other hands, what he craved most were a bath, a haircut and a shave. First he went into a store, and bought a new hat, flannel shirt, vest and pants. Then he had a haircut, shave and bath, and put the new clothes on. He then felt ready to embark on the next stage of his search for the killers.

His former companions on the drive having left him to seek the dubious pleasures of the gambling-houses and saloons, Billy started looking for the store and livery stable owned by Dan Sinclair's friend Mark Butler. He found it almost immediately. The store was on a main street, with the livery stable out back.

Billy dismounted, and went into the

store. Behind the counter was a girl of about eighteen, blonde and very pretty. She looked at him and smiled. Although Billy had matured considerably, both mentally and physically, since leaving the homestead, contacts with pretty young girls had been noticeably absent. He blushed slightly.

'Is Mr Butler around please?' he asked.

'He's round the back, in the stable,' she replied. 'You new in town?'

'Yes,' replied Billy. 'Got in today. I've just finished helping to drive a herd up from Texas.'

The girl studied him. She had seen quite a few cowboys in town from time to time, and Billy's behaviour didn't quite seem to fit into the usual pattern. She knew that the normal cowboy at that time, when paid off at trail's end, would, having bathed and shaved, have an irresistible urge to liquor up, mount his horse, and, with his comrades, dash through the main streets, yelling like an Indian, and firing his gun in the air.

But Billy didn't show any sign of being liquored up, she thought. Nor did he give any indication that he was about to start yelling. In fact he looked like somebody who, despite his youth, had himself well under control, and had less frivolous matters to attend to than shooting up the town. And what's more, she thought, he's a lot better looking than most cowboys I've seen.

'You can go out back and see pa if you like,' she said.

Billy found Mark Butler sweeping out the stable. He was a man in his mid-forties. He looked up as Billy approached.

'My name is Billy Dare,' said Billy. 'I'm looking for a job I can maybe do just for a month or two, and I may have to leave sudden-like. I've got a letter here for you from Mr Sinclair down in Texas. He thought that maybe you could help.'

Butler read the letter, then turned to Billy, and shook his hand.

'Dan says he's mighty beholden to you,' he said. 'He don't say why, and I ain't aiming to ask. Dan was a good friend to us, and I'm glad to help. It so happens I need a hand here at the livery stable. I had one until a week ago, but he joined up with a drover who was taking a herd up to Wyoming. If you want the job, and you figure you can handle it, it's yours. Try it out for a few days. You can bunk down in the stable. There's a bed over there.'

'Thanks,' said Billy. 'I'd like to take the job. I'm obliged to you.'

Billy quickly settled down to his work at the stable. They had had several horses on the homestead, and he had a natural liking for the animals, unlike the average cowhand, who looked on the cowpony merely as a tool of his trade, giving it little or no affection, and getting rid of it immediately when it was no longer up to the job.

The stable was well patronized, and what with cleaning up, and attending to the horses, and occasionally helping to handle goods in and out of the store, Billy was kept pretty busy. Butler indicated that he was more than pleased with Billy's work. When Billy got time off, he saddled up his bay, which Butler had agreed he could put up at the stable, collected a few empty tin-cans, and rode out of town for a session of gun-handling and target practice.

Butler's daughter Ruth was an only child, and a little spoilt by her parents. Her self-assurance showed the influence of an eastern education. As Billy had been invited by Mrs Butler to eat with the family, he saw quite a lot of Ruth, and after a while he grew more easy in her presence, and began to get just a faint inkling of how a young girl's mind works. At the time of Billy's arrival, Ruth already had a steady beau, whose name was Frank, the son of banker Colville, and who was looked on with favour by Mrs Butler as an admirable suitor for her daughter's hand. Butler was not so sure.

'I know he's got a good background, Martha,' he admitted to his wife, after Frank Colville's first formal call on Ruth, 'but he's got a shifty eye, and I just can't whip up a liking for him at all.'

'Rubbish, Mark!' said his wife. 'Pretty nearly any young man calling on Ruth would feel uncomfortable with you staring and glowering at him all the time. Frank probably thinks you're a bit weak in the head. And don't forget,' she added, 'that Ruth seems to like him, and she's the one who'll have to live with him if they get married.'

At the time of Billy's arrival in Ellsworth the town was booming. Day after day the stock-pens disgorged into eastbound wagons cattle which only a few days earlier had been on the trail. The streets were thronged with cowboys, paid off, and with money to burn. Saloons, gambling-houses and whorehouses were all doing a roaring trade.

One morning, Billy noticed that about a hundred yards down the street from the store a fair-sized tent had been pitched in a vacant space just off the main street. He walked along to see what new entertainment was about to be offered to the visiting cowhands, and the citizens of Ellsworth. As he approached the tent, he saw a board standing near the entrance, carrying the following announcement:

'*Doc Kibbee, the celebrated promoter, invites*

you to witness the amazing pugilistic prowess of the internationally famous Buster Mackay, who will take on all comers. Entrance two dollars.'

As Billy reached the tent, an elderly man, distinguished-looking, with a rather florid complexion, walked out. Billy assumed that this was Doc Kibbee. He was accompanied by a young man, in his twenties, who was dressed only in socks, shoes and a pair of tightly-fitting underpants. He was a handsome specimen of manhood, about five feet ten, with fair, curly hair, and well-muscled.

'Gather round, folks,' shouted the old man. His voice had a peculiar carrying quality, and he only had to repeat his invitation twice to attract a sizeable crowd in front of him, mostly cowhands.

'For the first time in Ellsworth, gentlemen,' he announced, 'I have the honour to introduce you to Buster Mackay, whose pugilistic prowess has made his name a household word. It is your good fortune, gentlemen, that he has tired of the idle and corrupt way of life back east, and

I have persuaded him to come west to demonstrate his pugilistic skill in an environment which produces a tough breed of men, well able to handle themselves, and frightened of no-one.'

He paused, and surveyed the crowd in front of him. He could see that he had their full attention. He continued.

'Inside the tent, gentlemen, is a roped-off ring where Buster will take on any opponent who wishes to challenge him to a fist-fight. Head-butting, wrestling and kicking are not allowed. Thirty dollars goes to any man who knocks Buster down for a count of more than ten seconds. The bout is over when either man is down for more than ten seconds, or when the challenger calls quits. And for the paltry sum of two dollars, gentlemen, you can have the privilege of viewing these contests. Please pay me as you pass into the tent.'

Billy joined the queue which lined up to enter the tent. It contained most of the Doc's audience, including all the cowboys, and filled the space around the ring. The Doc put up a board outside, chalked on it

'FULL HOUSE—NEXT SHOW 4 PM', went into the tent, and ducked into the ring, whose floor was covered with matting. Buster was already warming up. The Doc held up his hand for silence.

'Right, gentlemen,' he announced. 'We aim to put on a sixty-minute show if we have plenty of challengers. Who is going to be the first?'

A large cowpuncher, urged on by his comrades, ducked into the ring. He was tall for a cowboy, about six feet, with massive shoulders and long arms. He took off his hat and shirt, and without any further preamble he squared up to Buster. They circled for a few moments. Then the cowboy threw a right to Buster's chin. Buster moved his head away from the punch, and as the cowboy stumbled sideways, off balance, Buster threw in two left jabs to his opponent's ear. They were painful blows, and the cowboy, shaking his head, cursed, and launched himself at Buster, to find that, try as he might, he could not land a solid punch on his opponent. It seemed to Billy that

Buster was able to anticipate each of his opponent's moves almost before it actually started, and this, together with his nimble footwork, kept him out of his opponent's range. Growing more and more frustrated, the cowboy finally launched out on a mad rush at Buster, with his long arms outstretched, in an effort to get him in a bear-hug. Buster ducked sideways under the arm of his opponent, straightened up, and planted a straight right on the side of his opponent's jaw as he floundered past. The cowboy went down like a log, and it was well outside the allotted ten seconds before he was able to get up.

Billy had watched all this, enthralled. He had only ever seen one fist-fight between adults, and that was on the trail-drive when two trail-hands fell out. It had been a scrappy, fist-flying, bull-rushing affair, in which it seemed almost inevitable that the stronger participant must win. But Billy could see now that size and strength *could* be overcome by skill.

The next contestant was a tough, mean-looking character with a three-day stubble, and about the same size as Buster. As soon as the bout started, and the two men commenced circling, Billy could see that Buster's new opponent was considerably more skilful than his predecessor. His guard was more effective, his footwork seemed better, and he started off with a flurry of punches, a few of which landed on Buster's body. Buster seemed unconcerned, however, and was content for a time to keep out of harm's way with a skilful exhibition of foot-work and body movement. The audience grew restive, and yelled for more action. Buster's opponent was running out of steam, and growing more and more frustrated.

'Why the hell don't you stop dancing around, and fight like a man?' he snarled.

Buster obliged. He blocked his opponent's next punch, then with great speed and accuracy he jabbed him on the nose with his left, followed up, and before his opponent could recover, dropped him with a straight right to the jaw, the same punch which had floored his predecessor. Doc Kibbee counted the man out.

Billy had to leave at this point in the proceedings, as there was work to do in the livery stable. In the evening, after the second show was over, he walked over to the wagon standing near the tent. He could see Doc Kibbee and Buster sitting inside.

'Can I have a word with you, sir?' asked Billy, addressing the Doc.

'Get in,' invited the Doc, 'and go ahead.'

'My name is Billy Dare,' said Billy. 'I saw the show earlier today, and I've come to see if maybe you could show me how to fight like Mr Mackay.'

The Doc eyed Billy up and down.

'You hankering to join the show, boy?' he enquired.

'No,' replied Billy, 'but later this year I'm liable to meet up with some rough characters, and I figure I'd better be able to look after myself a bit better.'

'Can't you handle a gun?' asked the Doc.

'I can,' answered Billy. 'I've got a Colt .45. But I reckon a gun ain't always the answer when you're in trouble, and I sure would like to be able to fight like Mr Mackay.'

The Doc spoke to Buster, who had been eyeing Billy curiously.

'What do you think, Buster?' he asked. 'Can we make a fighting-man out of Billy Dare?'

'He's got the body for it,' replied Buster.

'Yes,' said the Doc, 'but has he got the brains?'

He thought for a moment.

'Tell you what,' he suggested. 'Let's all go in the tent, and you can spar with Buster for a while so's we can see how you shape.'

Fifteen minutes later, the Doc spoke to Billy.

'Well, Billy,' he said. 'You've got the build, and your footwork isn't bad, but your knowledge of the science of fisticuffs is obviously zero. However, we're here for another four weeks, and if you've got forty dollars to spare, we'll give you a session of training each day. I'm keeping the price down because a session with you each day will help to keep Buster in shape,

96

especially as you get better. When it's over, you should be able to look after yourself a sight better than you can now.'

'Thanks,' said Billy. 'I'll go and get the money.' Although the payment would make a big hole in his earnings from the trail-drive, he reckoned it would be worth it.

During the next four weeks, during his time off, Billy proved an apt pupil during the training sessions. Buster was a good-natured fellow, with endless patience, and Billy got on well with him. At the end of the last session, the day before the show was leaving Ellsworth, he bade the Doc and Buster farewell.

'I've got to say, Billy,' said the Doc, as Billy was leaving, 'I never figured you'd pick it up quite so quick. Buster's one of the best fighters I ever handled, and even he's beginning to find you a bit of a handful. You've got a very quick reaction, Billy, and that's a mighty big advantage for a boxer. But there's one thing you must do, and that is to get more power into your punch. If you rig up a punching-bag like the one Buster has been showing you how to use, you could work on that yourself.'

'I'll do that,' said Billy, 'And thank you both for your help.'

It was a few days later, while Billy, bare-chested, and sweating profusely in the heat, was in the middle of a session with the punch-bag, that Ruth Butler walked into the stable. She saw him attacking the bag with a ferocity which was entirely out of keeping with the placid temperament which he usually showed. He caught sight of her, and stopped abruptly.

'My goodness, Billy!' exclaimed Ruth. 'What a frightening sight this is. I had no idea you were such a fierce character.'

Billy dodged behind the punch-bag in confusion.

'Miss Ruth,' he said. 'It ain't right for you to see me like this—with no shirt on, I mean. What would your ma and pa say?'

'I don't know, Billy,' she replied, 'and I don't aim to find out. I came in here to find my pa. He isn't here, so I'm leaving. You can carry on with your foolish game. What are you doing, anyway?'

'Well, Miss Ruth,' explained Billy, peering around the punch-bag. 'I've been trying to learn a few things about fist-fighting, in case it might come in handy. I fixed up this punch-bag so I could strengthen up on my punch.'

'How disgusting!' exclaimed Ruth. 'All some people think about nowadays is fighting and brawling. I'm glad that Frank Colville's mind is set on higher things.'

She flounced out of the stable.

A few days later, around the same time, Billy was having his usual practice session on the punch-bag when he heard what sounded like a burst of high-pitched giggling outside the stable, followed by a man's voice, and the sound of running feet. Mark Butler walked into the stable. He saw Billy at the punch-bag.

'I'll never understand women, Billy,' he said, 'especially the young ones. I just found Ruth and that friend of hers Dora Skinner watching you through that window behind you, and both giggling fit to bust. Now just tell me what's so funny about a man punching a bag.'

'I don't know,' replied Billy, 'but I figure I'll put a piece of sacking over that window in future.'

'You do that, Billy,' said Butler.

August was not far away now, and Billy was making his plans against the possible arrival of the three men he was after. The first thing he had to do was to try to make sure that if his mother's killers came to Ellsworth, he found out about their presence as early as possible after their arrival. There were two livery stables where riders who were staying in Ellsworth for a short while would most likely leave their mounts. One of these was Butler's. The other, on the other side of town, belonged to a Brett Carrigan, a friend of Butler's, who had a man called Jim Rider running the place for him. Billy, with Butler's agreement, had helped Rider out for a few days while the latter was suffering from a damaged leg sustained in a fall. Billy and Rider, an ex-cowboy in his early thirties, had grown quite friendly, and looked in on each other occasionally.

Billy went over to see Rider, and took

him into his confidence, but asked him to keep to himself what he was being told. He told him about his mother's death, and explained that there were three men involved. He told Rider that one of the men was called Arnie, but whether this was his first or last name was not known. He was over six feet, fattish, with a black beard. The other two were slim, and of medium height, and one of them dragged his left foot. All three were tough-looking characters, and all three were wearing guns. Billy asked Rider to let him know right away if he saw anyone answering the descriptions he had been given. Rider promised to do this. Then he asked Billy what he intended to do if anyone turned up resembling the description of the killers.

'Well,' replied Billy, 'if a big, black-bearded man turns up together with a man dragging his left foot, then there's a good chance that these were two of the men described by the bartender in Little Bluff. What I have to do is to try and get proof of this, then I'll know they're two of the three men who were there when my mother was murdered. And if there's a third man with them, likely he'll be the third man who was there when my mother was killed. Sheriff Hart in Larraby was sure that the men seen in Little Bluff were the killers. He followed their tracks all the way from our homestead. Maybe I'll have a word with the law here about those three.'

'I think that's a good idea,' said Rider.

As Billy walked back towards the livery stable, he paused outside Ellsworth's premier saloon and gambling-palace. Seated in an armchair on the boardwalk outside the saloon was an old-timer, Bart Hunter, ex-wagon master and gold-miner. His working days were long over, and now, partially crippled by rheumatism, his main occupation was, from this vantage-point, to observe the comings and goings of both the transient and permanent populations of Ellsworth. Little escaped his notice. Billy, figuring he might feel a bit lonely sitting on his own out there, was in the habit of having a brief chat with the old man whenever he passed that way.

He walked over to Hunter.

'I was wondering if you'd do something for me, Mr Hunter,' he asked. 'There may be some men coming into Ellsworth sometime soon that I want to see. I don't know exactly when they're coming, and they don't know I'm here. Would you watch out for them, and let me know if you see them, please?'

'Sure will, Billy,' agreed the old-timer. 'What do they look like?'

Billy passed on all the information he had about the big man and his companions.

'There's just one more thing,' said Billy. 'I don't want them to know I've been looking out for them.'

'Right, Billy,' said Hunter. 'I see most people who ride in here, and if I spot the ones you've mentioned, I won't say anything to them, but I'll get word to you pronto.'

'Thank you, Mr Hunter,' said Billy, 'I'd appreciate that.'

The following day, Billy decided to have a word with the law about the three men he was after. After work, he walked along to the marshal's office. He found Deputy Marshal Dixon sitting inside, alone, and gave him a brief account of his reasons for being in Ellsworth, with descriptions of the men he was seeking. He asked Dixon if he could fit these descriptions to anyone he knew.

Dixon thought for a few moments. Then he shook his head.

'No, I can't from memory,' he replied, 'but I've got a pile of "wanted" notices in the desk here from almost any place you could think of. Why don't you look through them? They go back quite a ways.'

He opened a drawer in the desk, pulled out a large, untidy heap of 'wanted' notices, and handed them to Billy.

Billy was three-quarters way through the pile when he looked intently at the poster he had just picked up. It was dated nine months earlier, before the time his mother had been killed. It had been issued in Missouri. It read:

'Reward of 500 dollars each for the capture

of the following three men, wanted for murder and attempted bank robbery in the State of Missouri. The men are known associates of the Williams gang: Arnold (Arnie) Hoffman. About 38 years, six feet two inches, 230 pounds, black beard, moustache; Luke Pearce. About 37 years, five feet nine inches, 165 pounds, moustache, walks with limp; Abel Jones. About 34 years, five feet eight inches, 160 pounds.'

At the top of the poster were three indistinct pictures of the outlaws' faces.

Billy read through the poster twice, then handed it to Dixon.

'I'm sure that these are the three men I'm after,' he said. 'Everything fits.'

Dixon read the poster.

'From what you told me, it sure looks like it,' he agreed. 'Seems that maybe things went wrong for them during a raid, and they killed somebody. They were probably on the run when they killed your mother.

'Now listen to me, Billy,' he went on. 'If we see those three in town, we'll arrest them. I'll tell the marshal all about it. If you see them before we do, you come and find one of us. You needn't worry about the law not giving them what they deserve. Not when a woman has been murdered, anyways.'

He handed the poster back to Billy.

'You keep this,' he said. 'I've got some copies.'

When August had come and gone, without sight or news of the three men for whom he was searching, Billy grew more and more restless. He began to wonder whether he should remain in Ellsworth for the time being, or whether he should start riding, now that he had some more information on the men, in the hope that he might pick up their trail somewhere else. Then, one day, just as he had decided that it would be best to move on, a young boy ran in to say that Bart Hunter wanted to see him.

Billy quickly finished attending to a horse for a customer, then asked Butler if he could go out for a while. Just as he left the stable, heading for the saloon, he heard the sound of gunfire, then silence. He broke into a run. When he turned the corner leading to the front of the saloon, he saw two men lying on the ground, and two horsemen riding hell for leather out of town, headed south. One was on a bay, the other, a tall man, on a sorrel. He approached the two men on the ground. Neither was moving. One man was Deputy Marshal Dixon. The other was a man in his mid-thirties. There was a gun on the ground close to each of the two prone figures. As Billy drew closer he could see that both men appeared to be dead.

People were now approaching from all directions, to group around the bodies. Billy walked over to Bart Hunter, who was standing on the boardwalk outside the saloon. He saw Billy coming.

'Those three men you told me about, Billy,' he said. 'I reckon they could have been those two riding off there, and that man lying in the street. They rode up here from the blacksmith's down the street there, and when they got off their horses at the saloon here, I could see that one man was dragging his foot. It was quite a spell after they'd gone into the saloon before I managed to get a boy to run along and tell you I wanted you.

'When they came out of the saloon,' he went on, 'Deputy Marshal Dixon was walking down the other side of the street, and he took a good hard look at them. Then he came over and spoke to them. I couldn't hear what they were saying, but they all pulled guns on the deputy at the same time. He didn't stand a chance, but he got one of them before he went down.'

'Is the lame man one of the two who rode off?' asked Billy.

'Yes, he is,' answered Hunter. 'If you know who these men are, Billy,' he went on, 'hadn't you better let the marshal know as soon as he gets back? I saw him ride out of town this morning, but from what I heard he won't be away long.'

'The marshal will know who they are, Mr Hunter,' said Billy, 'if you tell him I'm pretty sure they're the three men that I was speaking to Deputy Marshal Dixon about a while ago. Will you tell him as well that I'm taking off after those two right away, before the trail gets cold?'

'I will,' promised Hunter, 'but take care, Billy. That's a dangerous pair to follow.'

Billy turned, and walked past the group standing around the two bodies, towards the livery stable. When he reached it, he spoke to Butler.

'There's been a shooting outside the saloon down the street,' he told him. 'Deputy Marshal Dixon has been killed, and an outlaw is dead. Two other outlaws have escaped. I've been looking for these men for a while now, and I'm going to get on their trail right away. I'm sorry if it puts you out, but I did say when you took me on that I might have to leave sudden-like.'

'That's all right, Billy,' said Butler. 'You've done a good job here, and I'm grateful. Is the marshal getting a posse together?'

'He's out of town just now,' answered Billy. 'I figure he'll do that as soon as he gets back. Meantime, I'm going to get on the trail of those two.'

'I guess you've got a mighty good reason for taking off after those men on your own,' said Butler, 'but for God's sake watch out for yourself, Billy.'

'That I aim to do,' replied Billy.

He saddled the bay, got some provisions and a water-bottle from the store, put on his gunbelt with the holstered Peacemaker, picked up his rifle, and walked his horse out of the stable. Butler and his wife and daughter were waiting outside to see him off.

'We're sorry to see you go, Billy,' said Mrs Butler. 'We've got used to seeing you around here. We'll all be wishing you well.'

'Thank you, ma'am,' said Billy.

He mounted, and rode down the street, then past the saloon where the recent gun-battle had taken place. The bodies had been removed. Bart Hunter was sitting in his usual place, and Billy gave him a wave as he passed. He rode on to the blacksmith's, and dismounted. The smith, Josh Forbes, was shaping a piece of red-hot metal on his anvil. He stopped when he saw Billy, who had brought him horses for shoeing from time to time, and laid the piece of metal down.

'Howdy, Billy,' he said. 'You hear about the shooting?'

'Yes,' replied Billy. 'I happened along just after those two men rode off. Bart Hunter was telling me that they were here before they went to the saloon.'

'That's right,' said the blacksmith. 'One of them was a big man, bearded, over six feet. He was riding a sorrel with a loose hind shoe. When I looked at it, I could see there was a little piece broken off, and I told him he needed a new shoe. He told me pretty sharp that the old one would do, so I just nailed it up tight for him. They were only here for a little while.'

Billy looked down at the soft ground where the smith usually stood horses for shoeing. His gaze swept back and forth several times over the jumble of hoofprints. Then he saw it—a clearly-defined print of a shoe with a missing piece. He pointed at the print.

'Is that the print of that shoe?' he asked.

The blacksmith peered down, and studied it for a moment.

'That's it,' he answered.

Billy stared at the print for a while, memorizing every detail.

'I expect the marshal would like to see that print when he gets back,' he suggested.

'You're dead right,' said Forbes, inverting a small, empty water-barrel, and carefully placing it over the print. 'I'll show it to him.'

Billy rode off south, in the direction taken by the two outlaws.

6

Three days later, Billy camped for the night on the northern boundary of the Nations, the Indian Territory, which stretched south to the Red River and Texas, and which he had crossed earlier in the year with the trail-herd. Since leaving Ellsworth, the tell-tale hoofprint of the big outlaw's sorrel had led Billy to the point on the border where he was now camped. He had lost the trail several times on hard ground, but since the outlaws seemed to be making a beeline for the border, he had been able, on each occasion, to pick up the trail again further on. He figured, from the sign, that he was about a day behind them. He had seen no indication of the posse coming up behind him. Maybe, he thought, the marshal had not returned to Ellsworth on the day of the shooting, and there had been a delay in getting a posse organized.

The following morning, Billy rode south into the Indian Territory, following the outlaws' trail.

It was just before midday the following day when he heard a faint burst of gunfire some way ahead. He paused, but could see nothing moving in the hilly country in front of him. Keeping a sharp lookout, he rode on more slowly for a mile or so, then he caught sight of a rider appearing over the top of a small hill about three hundred yards on his left. It was an Indian. He was alone, and moving very slowly, and even as Billy watched, he slumped forward over the neck of his mount, then fell to the ground.

Billy waited for the Indian to get up, but he showed no sign of movement. He closely surveyed the surrounding country in every direction. Then he drew his gun, turned off the trail he had been following, and warily approached the body on the ground. As he drew closer, he could see that the Indian was about his own age, and was daubed with war paint. The Indian's rifle lay on the ground nearby. The body

114

lay sprawled on the ground, close to a large, rough-surfaced boulder on which he had probably landed when he fell.

Billy, still holding his gun, dismounted, walked up to the body, and bent down over it. The Indian's eyes were closed, and he was breathing heavily. There was a severe bruise on the side of his head, showing a seepage of blood. Billy could also see a wound on the Indian's right side. It looked as though a rifle-bullet had passed right through, probably during the recent gunfire. Blood was flowing from the entry and exit holes. The Indian's hand was bloodstained, as though he had been trying to stop the flow of blood.

Billy figured that the Indian had fainted from loss of blood, causing him to fall off his horse. The head injury had probably occurred when his head hit the boulder during the fall.

Billy picked up the rifle, took the knife from the Indian's belt, and walked over to collect the pinto. He tethered the two horses, then hid the rifle and knife in a small patch of brush nearby.

He looked down again at the Indian. He thought of the Indian attack on the trail-herd, and the mangled remains of Hank. Then his mind went back to his stay with the old gunfighter Jim Walsh. Walsh had expressed to Billy some definite views about Indians, views which were not popular among most of his white contemporaries.

'The Indians were here long before the white man,' he had pointed out to Billy. 'Some were farmers, some were hunters following the buffalo herds, and some were just fighting-men. But the white man has spread from east of the Mississippi clear across to the Pacific coast, and has settled a lot of the good farming-land and cattle-raising country in between. And what's more, he has just about killed off the buffalo herds. The Indians have been outnumbered, and many of them have been pushed off the land which was the home of their ancestors. It ain't surprising that they feel a mite put out, and want to hit back.'

Billy looked south, in the direction taken

by the outlaws he had been trailing. Then he turned and looked down at the Indian, who was still showing no signs of coming to. Blood was still flowing from the wound in his side, and Billy guessed that if this was not stopped, the Indian would soon be dead.

Once again, Billy carefully surveyed the surrounding country, but could see no sign of movement. Then he took a clean spare bandanna from his saddlebag, took off the one he was wearing, and tied the two together. He tore a large piece off the tail of his shirt, and made a pad. He poured some water from his canteen over the bullet-wound, then applied the pad and held it firmly in position by tying the two bandannas tightly around the body. Then, using more water from his canteen, he bathed the wound on the Indian's head. Although it had obviously been a severe blow, the bleeding there had stopped.

The Indian still showed no signs of coming round. Billy got his blanket, folded it, and placed it under the Indian's head. He collected some brushwood, lit a small fire, brewed some coffee, and opened a tin of beans which he warmed over the fire. Then, squatting on the ground, with his eyes on the Indian, he ate some of the beans and drank some coffee. As he watched the wounded man, he guessed that he must be suffering from concussion, something which had happened once to a school-friend of his, who had injured his head in a fall.

Just as Billy was drinking the last of his coffee, the Indian stirred slightly, groaned, and his eyes opened. Seeing Billy, his hand went to his belt in search of his knife, and he tried to rise. Almost immediately, he collapsed on the ground again, and lay there, eyes closed, for several minutes. Then his eyes opened again. He looked at Billy. His face and eyes were expressionless. His hand went up to feel the wound on his head. Then he looked at his bandaged side, and felt it gingerly with his hand. He slowly eased himself up, and sat with his back against the boulder. Billy got up, and walked over to him with the water-canteen. He offered it to the Indian, who took it, drank sparingly, and handed it back. Then the Indian spoke, slowly and weakly.

'Me Little Hawk,' he said.

'Billy Dare,' responded Billy, pointing to himself.

He held out a plate of beans in front of the Indian. The Indian took a mouthful, slowly ate it, then waved the plate away.

'Little Hawk mighty sick,' he said, weakly. He leaned back against the boulder, and lapsed either into sleep or unconsciousness, Billy was not sure which. He eased him off the boulder, and laid him on the ground.

It was growing dark now, and Billy placed his blanket over the Indian, made up the fire, and lay on his side watching the injured man. From time to time he rose and walked over to look more closely at the Indian, who appeared to be breathing normally, though still not conscious.

It was just before dawn when Billy dozed off. He awoke with a start half an hour later, opened his eyes, and froze. Around him and the wounded Indian stood a circle of Indian braves, each with face and torso decorated with war paint. His knowledge of the Indian tribes was scanty, but he thought that the Indians around him, as well as the one he had been tending to, were probably Comanches.

Three of them carried rifles, two of which were trained on Billy. The rest had bows and arrows. They stared at him impassively. Then one of the braves fitted an arrow to his bowstring, and aimed it at Billy's chest. Slowly, he started to pull back the arrow. Billy was still wearing his gunbelt and the holstered Peacemaker, and he was just about to draw his gun when the wounded Indian stirred, opened his eyes, looked around, and then spoke. His voice was still weak, but carried authority. The brave released the arrow from the bowstring, and replaced it in the buckskin quiver. The two rifles trained on Billy were lowered.

The wounded Indian, pointing to the bandannas tied around his body, spoke to one of the braves who appeared to be the leader of the party. Both glanced towards Billy. Then the leader of the party made a signal and, shortly after, a further Indian appeared, leading a bunch of horses. The wounded Indian slowly rose to his feet. He seemed quite steady now, and his eyes were clear. He slowly walked over to his own horse, and mounted.

Billy walked over to retrieve the rifle and knife from the patch of brush, and offered them to their owner, who took the rifle and handed it to one of his companions. Then he took the knife, sheathed it, and looked at Billy. He raised his arm in salute, turned, and rode off with the party to the east.

Shortly after they had left, Billy picked up the outlaws' trail again, and followed it south through the Indian Territory. The following day his luck ran out. A widespread torrential rainstorm hit the area, and washed out the faint intermittent trail he had been following. He kept straight on in the same direction the trail had been leading him since it entered the Indian Territory, but when he passed out of the rainstorm area he failed to pick it up again, despite riding a considerable distance west, then east. He gave up, and headed for Red River Station, hoping that the outlaws had crossed the Red River at that point.

When he reached Red River Station around noon, he bought some provisions, a new shirt and a couple of bandannas. He asked around, but no-one there had seen the outlaws. It was probable, he thought, that wishing to avoid attention, they had crossed the river at some other point. Or maybe they were still in the Indian Territory. He decided to head south into Texas in the hope of picking up the trail again.

He struck lucky when he enquired at a small homestead several miles south-east of Red River Station. The homesteader said that two riders answering the descriptions of Hoffman and Pearce had called and asked for water two days before, and when they left they were riding south. Billy headed in the same direction, and several miles on he once again picked up the distinctive hoofprint of Hoffman's horse. He pressed on in an effort to cut down the distance between himself and the outlaws. Then, two days later, he failed to pick up the trail again after losing it on a long, unbroken stretch of hard ground. Guessing that the outlaws might have veered east or west, he spent two days in a fruitless effort to pick up the trail again.

By now, he figured, he was close to the boundary of the Circle T ranch, from which he had set out on the trail-drive earlier in the year. He thought of Dan and Lois Sinclair, and of the promise he had made them to let them know how he was progressing. He headed for the ranch-house. While there, he thought, he would find out whether anyone had spotted the outlaws.

7

As Billy approached the Circle T buildings, two armed men walked out of the bunkhouse. One was holding a rifle, pointed in Billy's direction. He looked pretty tense, as if he didn't need much of an excuse to start firing.

'That's far enough, stranger,' he said. 'What's your business?'

Billy reined in his horse. He recognized the man with the rifle as one of Sinclair's ranch-hands, a man called Corrigan, whom he had met very briefly on his previous visit. The other man he had not seen before.

'Just visiting,' replied Billy. 'I've come to see Mr and Mrs Sinclair.'

'Is that so?' said Corrigan. 'Just keep your hand away from that sidearm. Just now, we don't take kindly to strangers riding over our range.'

'Don't you remember me, Mr Corrigan?' asked Billy. 'I'm Billy Dare. I was here a few months ago.'

Corrigan started. He looked closely at Billy, then lowered his rifle.

'Damn me!' he exclaimed. 'I see who you are now, and you couldn't have come at a better time. Right now the boss needs all the help he can get.'

He spoke to the other hand.

'This here is the feller you've heard us talking about in the bunkhouse,' he said. 'He's the one who faced up to Connors and Manley, and gave them both just what they deserved.'

The two hands walked up to Billy as he dismounted.

'Mr Sinclair in trouble, then?' asked Billy.

'He sure is,' answered Corrigan. 'It's rustlers. But I reckon you'd better go and hear it all from Mrs Sinclair. She's up in the house there. We'll tend to your horse.'

Billy walked over to the ranch-house, and knocked on the door. It was opened by

Lois. Billy was shocked by her appearance. Her face was drawn, her eyes reddened. For a moment she did not recognize him. Then, in a choked voice, she called out his name. He could see that she was near to tears. She took his arm, and led him inside. They sat down.

'Oh, Billy,' she said. 'We're in deep trouble. Did the boys outside tell you about it?'

'No,' replied Billy.

'Well,' she said. 'It all started ten days ago. One of our hands was found dead on the northern boundary. He had been shot in the back. Dan had thought for a while that we were losing cattle, and he suspected that rustlers were operating in that area. He had made a rough check, and figured that cattle were definitely being taken. He rode up there with Sheriff Carter and three hands, to investigate the killing and the rustling. They found tracks of a sizeable bunch of cattle crossing the boundary, and heading north across the Diamond S range. They followed the tracks for a day after they had cleared the Diamond S range. Then they were ambushed by maybe a dozen men, and the sheriff and one of the hands were killed. Dan and the other two hands held them off until dark, but Dan was hit in the chest. They managed to slip away in the dark, and get back here, but Dan lost a lot of blood on the way. He'd never have made it without the help of those two hands.'

Her voice quavered slightly.

'The doc got the bullet out,' she went on, 'but Dan's in a pretty bad way, Billy. It's still touch and go. He's as weak as a baby. It's hard to see him like this.'

'Has anything happened since Mr Sinclair was shot?' enquired Billy.

'The deputy sheriff took a posse out to the spot where the ambush took place,' answered Lois, 'but they lost the tracks a few miles further north. They scouted around for a few days, but they couldn't find any trace of the cattle or the rustlers. Seemed like they had vanished into thin air. So they came back.'

'Has anybody any idea who these rustlers

might be?' asked Billy.

'No,' answered Lois. 'I have the glimmering of a suspicion myself, with nothing to back it up, of who might be behind it, but I haven't mentioned it to Dan yet.'

'What suspicion is that?' asked Billy.

'Well,' explained Lois. 'That ranch I mentioned, the Diamond S, on the other side of our northern boundary, is about a quarter as big again as our own. It was taken over about six months ago by a newcomer from the east called Carter Brent. I've only met him a couple of times, and though he acts like a perfect gentleman, I've got a feeling that there's a devious and ruthless character underneath all that gloss. It seems that he has ideas about expanding his operations, because he's already approached the owners of two small ranches in the area with offers for their spreads. Both these ranchers told him they didn't want to sell.

'I've just got a bad feeling about him, Billy,' she went on. 'I did hear that he's taken on some more hands lately. Some pretty tough-looking characters by all accounts. I just feel that maybe he's behind all this trouble.'

'Is Mr Sinclair up to seeing visitors yet?' asked Billy.

'He's pretty weak, Billy, as I said,' Lois answered, 'but I know he'll want to see you. Mary's sitting with him now. She's a good girl, and helps me a lot with him. She...'

Lois broke off, then continued.

'But I was forgetting, Billy,' she said, 'that you haven't met Mary. Not long after you left on the drive, my sister and her husband were both drowned in a riverboat accident back east. Mary is their only child, and there was no-one to take her in back there, so I brought her out here. I think she misses some of her friends, and the kind of life she led back there, but she's settled down pretty well. Come on,' she went on, 'let's go up and see Dan now.'

As they entered the bedroom, the girl sitting by the bed turned to look at them. She was slim and good-looking with brown hair and hazel eyes, a combination which even back east, where women were less scarce, had turned many a male head. Billy guessed she was in her late teens. She rose and came towards them.

'He's asleep at the moment,' she whispered.

'Mary,' whispered Lois, 'this is a good friend of ours, Billy Dare. Maybe you remember your Uncle Dan and me telling you about him?'

'I remember,' whispered Mary. 'I'm pleased to meet you, Mr Dare.'

'My pleasure,' whispered Billy.

He looked over at Dan, lying on the bed. The invalid's face was pallid. He looked as if the vitality had been drained right out of him. As Billy looked, Dan's eyes opened and, after a moment, he turned his head, and looked at Billy and the two women. His eyes widened.

'Can that be Billy Dare,' he asked, 'or am I dreaming?' His voice was barely audible.

Billy walked up to the bed.

'It's me, Mr Sinclair,' he replied. 'I'm very sorry to see you like this.'

'You heard what happened, Billy?' asked Dan.

'Yes,' answered Billy, 'and I've just been wondering if I can help out in any way. I know a bit more about handling cattle since I went on that trail-drive.'

'I've got to say I don't know what you'd be getting yourself into,' said Dan slowly. 'But I sure could do with another hand I can trust right now.'

His voice trailed off, and his eyes closed.

Lois led Billy from the room. Mary stayed behind. They went downstairs, and sat down.

'I'm afraid, Billy,' apologized Lois, 'that I've been so concerned with our own troubles that I haven't asked how things are with you. Did you meet up with those men you're after?'

'One of them is dead,' answered Billy. 'Shot by a lawman in Ellsworth. I picked up the trail of the other two in Ellsworth, and I lost it about twenty miles north of here. I've got a copy of a "wanted" poster for them, and I reckon I can pick their trail up again when I'm ready. In the meantime,

I'd like to help you out if I can.'

'We're already so much in your debt, Billy,' said Lois. 'Are you sure you want to take a hand in this? It could be a dangerous business.'

'I'm sure,' replied Billy. 'What do you want me to do?'

'Well,' answered Lois, after a moment's thought, 'the two men we lost were our most experienced hands. In fact, one of them was our top hand. I'd like you to take his place, and take charge of the crew until Dan is fit again. We know we can trust you, you can take care of yourself, and as you said, you've had some experience handling cattle. You're young, and it's a lot to ask, but I'd be very grateful if you'd take the job on.'

'How many hands have you now?' asked Billy.

'We have six, without you,' answered Lois.

'All right,' said Billy. 'I'll do the best I can to keep things running around here until Mr Sinclair's fit again. I ain't had any experience handling men, but I've seen how a trail boss operates, and maybe I picked up a few pointers from him. But how do you think the hands will take it?'

'I don't think that any of them is a natural leader, Billy,' answered Lois, 'and I'm sure there'll be no trouble after I've had a word with them. Three of the men have been on the range today, but they'll be back by now. Let's go over to the bunkhouse, and I'll have a word with them.'

They walked over to the bunkhouse. It was dark now. Lois knocked on the door. It was opened by Corrigan, who stepped outside. He looked startled.

'Can I come in, Jed?' she asked. 'I'd like a word with the boys.'

'Just a minute, Mrs Sinclair,' he said.

He went inside, and pushed the door to behind him. Moments later, Lois and Billy heard a minor commotion arise inside the bunkhouse. It was fully a minute before it subsided. Then Corrigan opened the door again. Lois and Billy entered. It was a typical bunkhouse interior, with characteristic aroma, walls pasted with newspapers and nineteenth-century pin-ups, and a general air of permanent untidiness. The men were all standing. Lois spoke.

'First of all, boys,' she said. 'Let me tell you that my husband is still pretty bad, but he's just about holding his own, and the doctor said this morning that he has an even chance of pulling through.'

She motioned towards Billy.

'Some of you have already met Billy Dare,' she said. 'He did us a good turn earlier this year. He's offered to help out until my husband gets on his feet again. I'm putting him in charge for the time being, so you'll take your orders from him.'

'Right, Mrs Sinclair,' said Corrigan, 'if that's what you want. And we're glad to hear that Mr Sinclair is holding on.'

'Thank you, boys,' said Lois.

Billy accompanied her back to the house. They entered and sat down.

'I'd be grateful if you'd bunk down in the house here, Billy,' said Lois. 'With Dan like he is, I'd feel a lot better if you were around during the night.'

'Right,' said Billy. 'I'll bring my things in later. I've been thinking,' he went on, 'about how we should tackle the situation we're in at the moment. At this time of year, we don't have a round-up or trail-drive to bother about, so apart from the odd jobs around here, it's mainly a matter of keeping an eye on the cattle out on the range. Like always, we've got to check that they're healthy, but now we've also got to check that they aren't being driven off by rustlers. At the same time, we've got to do our best to make sure we don't lose any more hands. Is that how it seems to you, Mrs Sinclair?'

'I'm sure you're absolutely right, Billy,' agreed Lois.

'Have you had any more cattle taken since Mr Sinclair was shot?' asked Billy.

'We don't think so,' replied Lois.

'Not surprising, I suppose,' said Billy, 'with that posse riding around like it has been.'

Lois rose.

'I'll have to leave you now, Billy,' she

said. 'I must spell Mary off. We've been taking it in turns to sit with Dan. But first I'll show you where to bunk down, then you can get something to eat in the cookhouse.'

The next morning Billy was up early for breakfast in the cookhouse with the six hands. After the meal he spoke to them, nervously at first, then with a growing assurance.

'I didn't come looking for this job,' he said, 'but I want to help Mr and Mrs Sinclair if I can. What we have to do is keep an eye on the cattle as usual, and keep a close watch for signs of rustling. You'll go out in twos, and if you spot anything suspicious you'll hightail it back to the ranch-house so that we can decide how to handle it. The last thing you do is to follow the trail of any missing cattle. We all know what a murderous lot we're dealing with. For the time being I'll stay around here myself.'

He spoke to Corrigan.

'That gang that shot Mr Sinclair,' he asked. 'Did you see any of them close up?'

'We didn't get a good look at any of them,' replied Corrigan. 'And the way they caught us, I guess we were a mite careless. The sheriff reckoned the rustlers were well ahead, but they must have doubled back to ambush us. The three of us were mighty lucky to get away.'

'You sure were,' agreed Billy, 'and from what I hear, Mr Sinclair was mighty lucky to have the two of you along with him to help him home.'

Billy went on to discuss with the hands the details of the patrols over the range. Then he made a request.

'When I was here last,' he said, 'nobody living around here saw me, except people on this ranch and Sheriff Carter, and he's dead. So nobody except you and Mr and Mrs Sinclair and their niece know that I'm the one who had the run-in with Connors and Manley. I'd like to keep it that way.'

Doc Kinkaid rode in from Grafton later that morning to have a look at Dan. After seeing him off, Lois came over to Billy, who was cutting some stove wood.

'It's good news, Billy,' she told him.

'The doc says Dan has turned the corner. The fever has gone down, and he's a lot better than he was yesterday. The doc says he should be fit again in a few weeks' time.'

'That's good to hear,' said Billy. 'Did the doctor bring any news from town?'

'Yes,' answered Lois. 'It seems that the Box R owner, Josh Sheridan, suspects that he's losing cattle, but he has no definite proof yet. Also Carter Brent of the Diamond S claims that he's losing cattle, and he's taken on more hands, as I told you before. The doc says he saw three of them in town the other day. A mean-looking trio, he said, all strangers, and wearing guns.'

When the hands returned that evening, they had seen no signs of rustling activities.

Later in the evening, Dan asked to see Billy. When Billy entered the bedroom, he could see the improvement in Dan's condition. His face was less pallid, and his expression more alert than on the previous day. His voice, though still weak, was quite audible.

'Lois told me how you're running things, Billy,' he said. 'I reckon you're doing exactly the right thing. I'm feeling better today, and I'm hoping it won't be too long before I can take over. In the meantime, we're mighty grateful to you for helping out.'

As Billy went downstairs, Lois called him over to the couch, where she and Mary were sitting.

'We're badly needing supplies from Grafton,' she said, 'and Mary wants a few things from the store. Would you take her over there in the buckboard tomorrow?'

'Sure,' said Billy. 'I'll be glad to.'

The next morning, he arranged for two of the hands to stay around the ranch buildings while he was away. Then he hitched up the buckboard. Mary came out of the house looking pretty as a picture. Under the envious gaze of the two punchers, Billy helped her onto the buckboard. Lois came out to see them off. She handed Billy a list of supplies.

'Dan's still getting on fine, Billy,' she reported. 'He's even asking for food this morning. I don't know if it's anything to do with you turning up, but he certainly has perked up since you arrived.'

Billy got onto the buckboard, and headed for town. The seat was narrow, and his close proximity to Mary made him a trifle self-conscious. For a short while they rode in silence. Then Mary spoke, with the assurance of a young lady raised and educated in the east.

'Since you're a friend of my aunt and uncle, I'll call you Billy,' she said, 'and you may call me Mary.'

'Yes, miss,' said Billy.

'From what Aunt Lois has told me, Billy,' went on Mary, 'you are a veritable knight in shining armour.'

'I am?' asked Billy, somewhat taken aback by the description.

'Yes,' answered Mary. 'After all, you did ride to the aid of the damsel in distress, didn't you?'

'If you're talking about me helping Mrs Sinclair out, the answer is yes,' said Billy. 'I was glad I happened along.'

'And now,' continued Mary, 'once again

140

you are coming to the rescue. I should think that friends like you are few and far between.'

'I was only aiming to help out a little while Mr Sinclair is out of action,' said Billy, embarrassed.

'Aunt Lois tells me that you are searching for some outlaws who murdered your mother. Will you carry on with that search when you have finished here?'

'I will,' answered Billy. 'I just figure that men like that shouldn't be allowed to stay free.'

Neither spoke again until they reached the outskirts of Grafton. Then Billy asked Mary where she wanted to go.

'Over to the dry-goods store over there, next to the saloon,' she answered, pointing, 'and you can get the supplies you want at the general store next door.'

Billy pulled up, and helped Mary down. She went into the dry-goods store, while he entered the general store with his list. He introduced himself to the storekeeper, Cal Harvey, who, after enquiring about Dan, consulted the list and started to pile up the wanted items near the door.

'Anything new in town?' enquired Billy.

'Nothing much,' replied Harvey. 'We've had a few strangers around lately. New hands taken on by the Diamond S. They ride into town from the ranch now and then. In fact there are three of them in the saloon there right now. The story is that Brent took them on because of this rustling business.'

Billy and Harvey loaded the supplies onto the buckboard. They had just completed this task when Mary came out of the dry-goods store, carrying two large parcels, and walked along in front of the saloon towards Billy and Harvey. As she did so, a man walked out of the saloon, and Mary, her view obstructed by the parcels in her arms, collided with him. The parcels fell to the ground.

The man was called Rafe Bennett. He was a professional gunfighter and, in his own estimation only, a lady-killer. He was of medium height, and stocky, with a slightly pockmarked face. He was dressed like a ranch-hand, and was wearing a gun.

His eyes widened as he got a good look at Mary.

'I'm sorry,' apologized Mary.

Bennett picked up the parcels, and handed them to her. He grinned.

'It was a pleasure,' he said, standing in front of her. 'It's a long time since I bumped into such a good-looking female. You live in town?'

'No,' replied Mary. 'I'm in a hurry. Would you please let me pass.'

She tried to walk around him, but, still grinning, he blocked her path.

Billy, who had observed the encounter, walked over and spoke to Mary.

'Everything all right, Miss Mary?' he asked.

Bennett, his temper flaring, turned on Billy.

'Back off, boy,' he said. 'Can't you see I'm talking to the lady.' Then suddenly, without warning, he gave Billy a violent push which sent him backwards over the edge of the boarded sidewalk, to land on his back in the street below.

Billy slowly got up, and stepped back

onto the sidewalk. Bennett moved up to him, and raised his hands with the intention of pushing Billy back again.

Billy got his feet in the right position, then put all the strength he had built up during his time at the punch-bag behind a hard right to Bennett's stomach. As Bennett doubled up in agony, Billy plucked the gunman's revolver from its holster with his left hand, and dropped it on the ground behind him. Then, as Bennett started to straighten up, Billy applied a replica of Buster Mackay's favourite knockout punch, a hard right-hander to the jaw.

Bennett fell off the sidewalk onto the street, where he collapsed on the ground. Instinct sent his hand to his holster, only to find that there was no weapon there. After a few moments, he slowly raised himself to a sitting position, and shortly after, he stood up, holding his stomach and swaying slightly.

'Damn you!' he said.

The saloon doors opened, and two men came out. They, too, were dressed as ranch-hands, and were wearing guns. One

144

was tall, the other around medium height. They stopped short as they saw Bennett.

'What the hell happened to you, Rafe?' demanded the taller of the two.

'Never mind that now,' said Bennett. 'Just give me a hand to teach this feller a lesson.' He pointed to Billy.

The three men advanced on Billy.

'Hold it!'

The shouted command came from the town marshal, who was approaching the group, and who could see that trouble was imminent. He walked between Billy and the three men facing him, and stopped.

'What's going on here?' he demanded.

'I saw it all, marshal,' answered Harvey, and described what had occurred.

'Lucky I happened along,' commented the marshal, when Harvey had finished. 'Do you want me to hold the man who was bothering you, miss?' he asked Mary.

Mary shook her head.

The marshal turned to the tall man.

'You men all from the Diamond S?' he asked.

The tall man nodded.

'I want you all out of town right now,' ordered the marshal. 'There's no place for troublemakers here.'

Bennett picked up his gun, then all three men mounted and rode off.

The marshal turned to Billy and Mary.

'How is Dan?' he asked.

Mary answered.

'The doctor says he's over the worst, and out of danger, but it will be a few weeks yet before he's in the saddle again.'

'That's good news,' said the marshal. 'Now I'd like you to pass some news on to him. I just heard from the new sheriff, Sheriff Lang, that is, that Josh Sheridan has been found dead, out on the range, by one of his men. Maybe you know that Josh ran the Box R spread, next to Dan's. Like Dan, he figured he was losing beef, and he was checking up in that area. He was a darn fool to go out there alone.'

'Has the sheriff got any ideas about what's happening?' asked Billy.

'Since it seems that Josh Sheridan and Dan, and Carter Brent as well, have all been losing cattle,' answered the marshal,

146

'he figures that a biggish gang of rustlers is operating from somewhere north of here. He also figures that maybe they're driving the cattle clear up into the Indian Territory.'

'I'll give Mr Sinclair the news,' said Billy.

When they arrived back at the Circle T, Billy went to see Dan. Lois was sitting with him. Billy passed on the marshal's message. Dan lay quiet for a few moments. Then he spoke.

'This is beginning to look a bit more than a few hit-and-run cattle raids,' he commented. 'We ain't had anything like this before. Maybe we've lost a few steers from time to time, but we've never had any organized rustling on a big scale in these parts.

'Josh Sheridan was a good friend and neighbour,' he went on. 'His wife died a few years back, and he has no children. I'm wondering what will happen to his ranch.'

'I know,' said Lois, who had listened intently as Billy passed on the marshal's message.

147

'*You,* Lois?' said Dan. 'How could *you* know?'

'Carter Brent will get it,' said Lois. 'He'll buy it.'

'Carter Brent!' exclaimed Dan. 'Now I told you, Lois, when we were talking about it earlier today, to get the fool notion out of your head that Carter Brent is behind all this. Just because you didn't take to him when he took over the Diamond S. You know he's losing cattle the same as we are.'

'But *is* he?' asked Lois. 'We only have his own word for that.'

'Now Lois,' asked Dan, 'is there an ounce of real proof that Brent is involved in this killing and rustling?'

'Maybe not,' replied Lois, 'but I've got an instinct that doesn't often let me down, and that instinct tells me that he is.'

Seeing that Dan was tired, Lois dropped the subject.

Two weeks later, Dan was out of bed, and ten days after that he was in the saddle again. Two of the hands had ridden in to report signs that cattle had recently been driven off over the north boundary. Lois and Mary had ridden into Grafton for the day, escorted by two of the hands, and Dan had decided to ride out with Billy to the place where the cattle had crossed over, to have a look around.

At first, Billy demurred.

'It's probably just what they want you to do,' he pointed out.

'I'm damned if anybody is going to keep me off my own range,' responded Dan. 'But don't worry, Billy. I learnt my lesson last time. Nobody's going to ambush me again. We'll keep our eyes well peeled.'

'Let's go,' said Billy.

When they reached the north boundary, they soon located the spot where some cattle had been driven over. They dismounted, to look at the sign more closely. Then Billy, glancing to the north, saw three riders in the distance, cantering towards them.

'Three riders coming,' he called to Dan. 'What do we do? Hightail it back home?'

'We stay here,' replied Dan. 'It's like this, Billy. There's got to be a showdown sometime, and if we wait for another day, the odds against us may be a lot higher. So if you're with me, I'm staying put.'

Billy looked at the riders again. They were approaching three abreast.

'If there's trouble, you take the right-hand one,' he said to Dan.

'Right,' said Dan.

They stood, a few feet apart, with Billy on Dan's left, watching the three riders approach. As they drew closer, Billy saw that they were the three Diamond S men he had encountered in Grafton recently.

'They're Brent's men,' he told Dan. 'The ones I saw in Grafton.'

The three men stopped and dismounted several yards in front of Dan and Billy. As Billy had noted in Grafton, each man carried a gun in a low, tied-down holster. The one called Bennett looked hard at Billy for a moment.

'Well, well,' he said. 'If it ain't the kid who took my gun in Grafton. Nobody takes my gun and gets away with it. There ain't no lawman here for you to hide behind.'

150

'That's enough of that talk,' said Dan sharply. 'I'm Sinclair of the Circle T. What do you men want here?'

The tallest of the three answered. His eyes were cold.

'It's you we want, Sinclair,' he replied. 'You were lucky last time. This time you ain't got a chance. Neither has that sassy kid you've got with you.' He paused. 'Brent sure had you all running around in circles,' he went on. 'Blaming the killings onto rustlers, and running off your cattle himself. Looks like he'll end up with the Box R and Circle T spreads just like he planned. You've got to admire the man.'

The hands of the three Diamond S men hovered near their gun handles. The tall man was standing opposite Dan, Bennett was opposite Billy, and between them was the third man. Professional gunmen all three, to them the outcome of the impending gun-battle was a foregone conclusion.

They moved slightly apart. As they did so, the thought flashed into Billy's mind that it was almost a certainty that he and

Dan would be the targets for the first shots from the two men directly opposite them. The man in the middle would aim either at himself or Dan. If he aimed at Dan, then Dan's chance of survival, with two men firing at him, would be slim.

Billy decided that the man in the middle must be eliminated first. He made his draw, and shot the man in the chest before his victim had levelled his gun. As Billy fired, he ducked, and took a couple of quick steps to his left, so that Bennett just missed the moving target. Billy's second shot struck Bennett in the head.

The tall man beat Dan to the draw, but the unexpectedness of Billy's lightning draw and following movements distracted him slightly, and his first shot nicked Dan's ear, just before Dan fired a shot which grazed his opponent's shoulder. The tall man quickly cocked his gun again, but before he could pull the trigger to fire again, Billy's third shot struck him in the chest.

Holding his damaged ear, Dan peered

incredulously through the drifting gun-smoke at the three prone figures on the ground in front of him.

'My God, Billy,' he gasped. 'It beats me how you get that gun out so quick. And how the blazes you manage to shoot straight while you're dodging around like that, I just can't figure. I sure am glad you're on our side.'

They walked up to the three bodies. Billy kept them covered, while Dan checked them over.

'They're all dead,' he said. 'So Lois was right. Now that we've got the proof that Brent is behind the rustling and the killings, we'd better get to the sheriff as quick as we can, and tell him what we know. We'll leave the bodies here, and send somebody out from town to collect them.'

When they reached Grafton, they first found Lois and Mary and the two hands, and told them what had happened, and to stay in town. Then they headed for the sheriff's office.

Sheriff Lang listened to what they told

him with growing astonishment.

'Brent sure had us all fooled,' he commented, when they had finished. 'Do you think he knows yet that the game is up?'

'It all depends,' replied Dan, 'on whether the three men we tangled with have been found. He sent those men out to kill me, and when they're found dead he'll know he's finished.'

'I'm going to get a posse together right away,' said the sheriff, 'and we'll head for the Diamond S. We'll pick up some Box R men on the way.'

'Billy and I will go along with you,' offered Dan, 'and there are two more hands of mine in town who'll be going as well.'

When the posse arrived at the Diamond S, it seemed that Brent had not yet learnt that the three men he had sent out after Dan were dead. They found him and his foreman Gannon in the ranch-house, and took them without a struggle.

The marshal took Brent and Gannon into town, leaving some men behind.

'I figure,' he explained to Dan, 'that Brent must have sent the rest of his hands out on some job or other—maybe another rustling operation. Any of them who find out before they get back that the game is up will scatter in all directions, but there may be some who don't find out. That's why I want some men to lie in wait here for the time being.'

A few days later, Dan rode into town. When he returned, he came over to Billy.

'I've got some interesting news, Billy,' he said. 'I saw the sheriff in town this morning. You know that Brent's men took cattle from the Circle T and Box R ranges. Well, the sheriff says that Brent's foreman Gannon has been talking, and he says that the cattle have been driven up north, about ten miles over the border into the Indian Territory, and Brent figured to drive them into Kansas later, or maybe bring them back here if he got hold of the Box R and Circle T ranches. There are some men, maybe three or four, holding them in a valley up there. The latest batch, about thirty head it was, left here the day before we had that brush with Brent's men on the north boundary. Gannon said there were two men driving those cattle north.'

'Did he say who the two men were?' asked Billy.

'According to the sheriff they were two hands that Brent took on a few weeks ago,' answered Dan. 'He told me their names. One of them sounded like a German name, Hoffman I think it was, and the other was Pearce.'

Billy stiffened.

'I'm going to see the sheriff,' he said. 'Those are the names of the two killers I'm after. I've got to check if they're the same men.'

'Most likely they are,' said Dan. 'You said you lost their trail near here. They were probably heading for Brent's spread at the time.'

When Billy reached town, he found the sheriff in his office. He showed him the 'wanted' poster which the lawman in Ellsworth had given him. He asked him if he could say whether the Hoffman and Pearce on the poster were the same men who had taken the cattle north.

'They are,' answered the sheriff. 'So happens I met up with them in town one day, and got a good look at them. Why are you so interested in them?'

Billy told the sheriff the story of his mother's death.

'Pity I didn't know they were wanted when I saw them in town,' said the sheriff. 'I guess they'll be out of my jurisdiction by now, but if they come back this way, I'll take them in for murder. Gannon didn't know the exact place those cattle are being held,' he went on, 'but he knows Brent gave Hoffman and Pearce a map showing them just where to go. Judging by the direction the rustlers were taking when Sheriff Carter and Dan Sinclair were ambushed, I figure they were heading for some place east of the Chisholm trail. I've heard there are plenty of places in that area where stolen cattle or horses can be hidden. I've notified the US Marshal in Fort Smith, Arkansas, about the rustlers and the stolen cattle, and they'll be on the lookout for them. And by the way,' he added, 'there's one thing about Hoffman that poster didn't mention. I noticed the top of his right ear is missing. Probably shot off.'

Billy rode back to the ranch, and told Dan what had transpired.

'This means you'll be leaving us soon?' queried Dan.

'Tomorrow,' answered Billy. 'I'm hoping maybe I'll find Hoffman and Pearce at the place the stolen cattle are being held.'

'You want to take some men with you?' asked Dan.

'No,' declined Billy. 'I've got a better chance of sneaking up on them on my own. If I get in a situation where I want help after I've located those rustlers, I'll try and get word to you.'

'Right,' agreed Dan.

8

Billy set off the following morning. Lois and Dan saw him off.

'Take care, Billy,' entreated Lois, 'and always remember that there's a home here for you whenever you want it.'

'Good luck,' said Dan.

Billy headed north, across the Diamond S range, and on to the spot which Dan had described to him as the place where he had been ambushed and shot. Then he headed straight for the Red River, which he reached at a point east of Red River Station. He rode eastward along the bank for a while until he found a good crossing-point. He could see signs of a few cattle on the south bank. He crossed over to the north bank. There were further recent signs of cattle there, once again not in large numbers. Some of the tracks led north, and some east. It was impossible to say whether any of the tracks belonged to the cattle Hoffman and Pearce had been driving. To the west the terrain was fairly flat as far as he could see. To the east was more rugged country. Somewhere in there, he suspected, were the stolen cattle. Up to the north, he could see a line of low hills in the distance. Suddenly, as he surveyed the terrain, the task of finding the rustlers seemed insuperable. There must be, he thought, hundreds of small valleys and ravines in which the cattle might be hidden.

His fit of pessimism soon passed. He was reasonably certain that the hiding-place was around ten miles north of the Red River, so he decided to ride about ten miles north of his present position, then to head in an easterly direction parallel to the river, diverging where necessary in order to inspect any possible hiding-places. He knew that caution was necessary, because the sheriff had told him that criminals were hiding out in many parts of the Indian Territory, and they did not take kindly to strangers.

He had been riding half an hour, without seeing anything of interest, when he spotted a saddled horse grazing just outside the entrance to a small canyon. He stopped his mount, and looked around, his hand on the handle of his Colt. He could see no sign of the owner of the horse. Keeping clear of the canyon's entrance, he rode up the slope to near the rim of the canyon, dismounted, and crawled forward to look down into it. Not twenty yards away, just inside the canyon entrance, near the foot of the slope leading to the canyon floor, a man was lying, partly covered by loose rocks and earth. He was groaning. His gun had fallen out of its holster, and was lying on the slope a few feet away from him. He did not see Billy. Billy looked up the canyon. No-one else was in sight. He went back to his horse, mounted it, and rode down to the canyon entrance, into the canyon, and up to the fallen man.

As the man caught sight of him, he scrabbled frantically in a vain effort to get hold of his gun, then collapsed with a shout of pain. He was a small man, with a straggly grey moustache, and a weather-beaten face. He looked to be in his sixties. As Billy dismounted, the man inspected him closely.

'You don't look like the law,' he said.

'I ain't,' said Billy. 'You busted something?'

'It's my leg,' groaned the man. 'Like a fool, I was riding down the slope here when the rocks and soil started moving. My horse fell, and rolled over my leg. I can move it, but it hurts like hell. I got a knock on the head too. Only came to a minute ago. Dunno where my horse is.'

'It's grazing just outside the canyon there,' said Billy. 'Looks all right to me.'

'That's one good thing then,' said the man, relieved. 'I like that horse. Name's John Murdoch, by the way. I was out looking for a stray horse.'

'Billy Dare,' said Billy. 'You living near here?'

'Me and my partner Brett Jardine have a little shack about two miles east of here,' replied Murdoch.

Billy knelt down, and cleared the loose

stones and earth from around Murdoch. Murdoch bent forward, and passed his hand around his right leg a few times.

'Can't feel any broken bones,' he commented. 'Maybe it's just crushed. Whatever it is, I sure can't walk.'

'You think you can ride if I get you on your horse?' asked Billy.

'I reckon I could manage a couple of miles,' grunted Murdoch.

Billy went to collect Murdoch's horse. He inspected it closely. There were no injuries that he could see. He led the horse up to the injured man and helped him up, then lifted him so that he could place his left foot in the stirrup. Murdoch then pulled himself up, and eased his bad leg over the saddle. He made no sound, but Billy could see the beads of sweat on his brow, and he guessed that the old man was in considerable pain. They rode slowly, so as not to jar Murdoch's leg, and it was an hour before the old man turned his horse into the entrance of a small canyon, and stopped just before he got inside. Then, despite the pain he was obviously in, he gave a tolerable imitation of the call of a coyote.

'Just a signal to my partner,' he explained, then moved on into the canyon, which opened out as they moved forward. There was a shack, about a hundred yards away on the left, just beyond a small corral holding twelve horses. Billy guessed that they were stolen. A man came out of the shack, saw that Murdoch had company, and went in again, to emerge a moment later with a rifle. He looked about the same age as Murdoch, but was a larger man, and bearded.

'That's Brett,' said Murdoch.

Jardine held the rifle on Billy as they approached.

'Put that rifle away, Brett,' said Murdoch, as they came to a stop. 'This young feller is Billy Dare. He just did me a good turn. Horse rolled on me and bust my leg. Billy helped me get back here.'

He turned to Billy.

'This is my partner Brett Jardine,' he said. 'Brett's a good man to have around if you get hurt. Worked in an army hospital for a while. He'll fix me up good in no time.'

They helped Murdoch down, and onto a bed inside the shack. There was a look of concern on Jardine's face, and Billy guessed that the two men were pretty close, and had been partners for some time. Jardine carefully pulled off Murdoch's pants, and closely examined his leg.

'I'm pretty sure,' he commented, when he had finished, 'that no bones are busted, and the skin is hardly broken, but that horse rolling over it hasn't done your leg any good at all. You're going to be laid up for a few days, John.'

'I figured I might be,' said Murdoch.

Billy accepted when Murdoch invited him to stay the night, and as soon as Jardine had made his partner comfortable, they had supper. It occurred to Billy that the two men probably knew the surrounding area intimately, and that they might be able to help him in his quest. On the other hand, if they were lawbreakers themselves, they might not be too keen to pass on information about rustlers in the area. All the same, he felt sure that they were not basically evil men, and certainly not killers. So he told them what he was looking for, and why he wanted to catch up with the two men Hoffman and Pearce.

'Is that man Hoffman a big man, surly-looking, over six feet, with a beard?' queried Murdoch, when Billy had finished.

'Yes, he is,' answered Billy.

'I knew him back in Arkansas, then,' recollected Murdoch. 'Never had any dealings with him. He was in with the Williams gang. They specialized in stagecoach and bank robberies.'

Murdoch continued.

'Brett and I ain't no saints, Billy,' he admitted, 'but robbing and murdering a decent woman in her own home is something else. Even if I didn't owe you a favour, I'd like to help if I can.' His anger appeared genuine.

'That goes for me too,' said Jardine.

'Well then,' said Billy, 'the cattle I just told you about are somewhere in this area, ten miles or so north of Red River.

Probably a few hundred head are being held. They started arriving about three months ago, and the last instalment would get here probably just over two weeks ago. Hoffman and Pearce were driving them.'

'It ain't healthy to pry into other people's business around here,' observed Murdoch, 'but as far as I know there ain't all that many cattle being held around here. There ain't many places with good grazing. All the same, maybe I can help,' he continued. 'Two and a half weeks ago, I was about five miles east of here, bringing two horses in, and I spotted two men quite a ways off, driving a small herd into a canyon. They didn't see me, and I swung round to give them a wide berth. That's all I know about any cattle around here.'

'I ain't seen any signs of cattle myself,' offered Jardine, 'and I reckon the men John saw could be the ones you're after.'

'Could you tell me how to get there?' asked Billy.

'Sure can,' agreed Murdoch, 'but I'd better draw it out for you. It ain't easy for a stranger to find his way around in these parts. Fact is, for a long time I used to get lost myself pretty regular. Get me a pencil and some paper, will you, Brett.'

When these were produced, Murdoch drew a rough map for Billy, showing the landmarks on the way to the canyon into which he had seen the cattle being driven.

'Now you know, Billy,' warned Murdoch, 'they're bound to have lookouts at the place those cattle are being held. Have you got any plans about what you're going to do when you get there? From what you say, you'll be up against three or four men, or maybe more.'

'I'm just going to look around first,' explained Billy, 'and find out if those cows really are from the Circle T and Box R. If they are, then I'll get help from those two ranches, and with a bit of luck, we'll get the cattle back, and capture Hoffman and Pearce at the same time.'

'You won't bring anybody near here, will you, Billy?' asked Murdoch anxiously. 'Brett and me are both real nervous of strangers.'

'You can count on that, Mr Murdoch,' promised Billy. 'I'm grateful for all the help you've given me. Could you tell me,' he went on, 'if there's a good cattle-crossing on the Red River east of here, but not too far away?'

'There's a good one about twelve miles east of here,' replied Murdoch. 'We use it often. Here, let me mark it up on that map I just gave you.'

When Billy woke the next morning, Jardine had his breakfast ready. Murdoch was eating his.

'How's the leg, Mr Murdoch?' asked Billy.

'A mite better,' the old man replied. 'Now don't go and do anything foolish when you get there, will you?'

'I won't,' said Billy.

'No need for you to leave here till around noon,' suggested Murdoch. 'You don't want to arrive there during daylight.'

Billy left around noon, and headed east. He moved slowly, keeping a sharp lookout, and frequently consulting the map which Murdoch had drawn for him. It was

169

growing dark when he stopped, about a mile from a large and peculiarly shaped outcrop which Murdoch had told him was close to the canyon entrance. He thought of Murdoch's warning about lookouts, and decided to stay where he was until it was really dark. When he set off again, he soon picked up the outline of the outcrop against the sky, and headed for it at a walk. When he reached it, he took his horse into a large cleft in the outcrop, where it would be hidden from the view of any lookout in the vicinity of the canyon. He stayed in the cleft, with his horse, until daylight. When he had breakfasted, he took from his saddlebag a pair of field-glasses which Dan had handed to him as he left the Circle T. He came out of the cleft, and climbed up the outcrop on the side remote from the canyon, circled round, and found a place where he could lie concealed, with a clear view of the whole canyon area.

So far as he could tell from his position, the canyon into which Murdoch had seen the cattle driven was very short, and appeared to lead into a large, oval-shaped and steep-sided valley, the bottom of which he was unable to see. Through the glasses, he studied the whole area closely, but could see no sign of a lookout. Then, as he looked once again along the top of the canyon, he thought he saw a movement behind a large boulder perched near the canyon rim. He kept his glasses on the boulder, and a minute later he saw a man step out from behind it, and stand with his back against it. He was carrying a rifle. After a short while, the man moved behind the boulder again, out of sight. Billy kept the whole of the area under observation for the rest of the day. Several times, he saw movements at the lookout position he had spotted earlier, but he could see no sign of a lookout at any other point. He concluded that only one lookout was being used.

After dark, he left the outcrop, and worked his way round on foot to the top of the slope leading down into the valley, keeping well clear of the lookout's position. He looked down into the valley. He could see lights in a small shack probably being used as living-quarters by the rustlers. He listened for a moment, then carefully made his way down the slope to the valley bottom. In the darkness, he could dimly see a small group of cows in front of him. He walked up to them. They were bedded down, but stood up as he approached. He hummed a night-guard lullaby, and walked to the side of the group of cows which was remote from the shack. Still humming the lullaby, he risked lighting a match, holding it in his cupped hands. As the cows moved away from him, he opened his hands momentarily, and caught a brief but clear glimpse of the Circle T brand on the nearest cow.

He quickly extinguished the match, and made his way over to the shack. He badly wanted to find out, before he left, if Hoffman and Pearce were there. As he neared the shack, he could hear two men talking loudly inside, and in order to hear the conversation better, he moved around near to the window, and stood listening. Then, totally unexpectedly, he felt the muzzle of a Colt jammed against the back of his neck, and his own Peacemaker was

172

pulled out of its holster.

'Make a move and you're finished!' growled a voice behind him.

Billy froze.

'Now walk round to the door, slow-like,' ordered the man, still jamming the Colt into Billy's neck. When they reached the door, the man banged on it with Billy's Colt.

'Pete here!' he shouted. 'We've got a visitor. Open up!'

The door opened, and the two men inside stared at Billy as he was pushed into the shack.

'Search him, Roy,' ordered the man behind Billy.

One of the two men in front of Billy moved up to him, and searched him thoroughly. Then the man behind him pushed him across to the far corner of the shack, and ordered him to turn round. Billy had a good look at the three men. None of them was Hoffman or Pearce.

'Now, Roy,' ordered the man called Pete, 'you go and see if everything's all right at the lookout. And you, Bud, have a scout around, and see if we've got any more visitors. I'll keep an eye on this one.'

The two men returned after twenty minutes, to report that all was well.

'Good,' said Pete, relieved. 'It was a good thing,' he went on, 'that I had a hankering to bed down early tonight outside. If I hadn't, I wouldn't have seen this feller taking a look at the brands on them cows.'

'Looking at the brands!' exclaimed Bud.

'That's what I said, Bud,' confirmed Pete. 'What else would he be doing standing in the middle of the herd with a lighted match?'

The three rustlers studied Billy closely.

'Don't look like no lawman to me,' observed Bud.

'You're right,' said Pete. 'I can smell a lawman a mile off, and this feller ain't one of them.'

He spoke to Billy.

'You got a mind to tell us what you're doing here, feller?' he asked.

'No,' answered Billy, who couldn't think

up any lie which could possibly convince the three that his arrival there was pure chance. All he could do was to play for time, in the hope that the opportunity to escape might arise.

'Maybe we can change your mind for you,' suggested Pete. 'We've got a man coming in tomorrow who's a specialist in getting information out of fellers like you. He learnt a few tricks about torture from the Indians, and gets quite a kick out of trying them out. I guess we can wait till he gets back. He'd be mighty put out if we had a go at you before he did. Tie his hands and feet, Bud,' he went on, 'and sit him in the corner there.'

Billy was wondering if the fact that he hadn't seen Hoffman or Pearce meant that they were the one on lookout, and the one returning the following day. He knew this was not so when Bud went to relieve the lookout, and the man he had replaced came into the shack. The man was neither Hoffman or Pearce. He looked curiously at Billy.

'Dunno how he got in,' he said. 'He

didn't come through the canyon, I'll swear to that.'

'I think you're right, Jim,' agreed Pete. 'I reckon he came down the slope into the valley. But we can't watch everywhere. Main thing is, we've got him. When it's daylight, you go out and see if you can find his horse. It must be somewhere near.'

The three men sat down at the table, and Pete produced a bottle of whisky and three battered mugs. He poured drinks for the three of them.

'Hoffman and Pearce should be back with some more cattle in two or three weeks' time,' he said. 'So maybe...'

He paused, as Roy pointed towards Billy.

'Whatever he hears here, he sure ain't going to pass on to anybody else,' said Pete. 'I was going to say,' he went on, 'that maybe Brent will send word how much longer we have to stay here, and where we've got to drive those beef. I'm getting a bit tired of hanging around in The Nations.'

As Billy listened, he realized that news of

Brent's downfall had not reached the men at the table. He also realized that while he was riding North, Hoffman and Pearce had been riding south. Possibly they had passed within a few miles of each other. He wondered whether the two men had been caught when they reached the Diamond S. He listened again to what the men at the table were saying.

'Can't say I took to that man Hoffman,' commented Roy. 'He ain't got no manners at all. Eats like a pig, and looks at you like he thinks you're dirt.'

'Whatever you think about Hoffman, you'd better keep to yourself when he's around,' warned Pete. 'For a start, he's a lot bigger than you, and second, I've never seen a faster man with a gun. I saw him in some shoot-outs down in Texas a few years ago. And he's mean, real mean. I once saw him nearly strangle a man with his bare hands, just because of an argument over a game of cards. Rile him, and anything can happen.'

'You know anything about his partner, Pearce?' asked Roy.

'They've been together for a long time,' answered Pete. 'Pearce ain't so fast as Hoffman with a gun, but there ain't much in it. That's a real dangerous pair, I can tell you. There was a third man rode with them, Jones I think his name was. Dunno what's happened to him.'

He yawned.

'I'm going to turn in now,' he said. 'One of you check the ropes on his hands and feet before you do the same.'

Billy slept as well as he could, with hands and feet tied, and lying on the floor. When breakfast was on the go, Pete told Jim to untie Billy's hands, and give him some food and coffee. When he had finished the meal, Billy's hands were tied again. Jim left the shack, and returned some time later.

'Found his horse,' he told Pete, 'behind that big outcrop.' He held up the field-glasses. 'These were in his saddlebag. Guess he's been spying on us. No sign of anybody else out there.'

'You didn't find anything to tell us who he is, or what he's doing here?' asked Pete.

'Not a thing,' replied Jim.

Pete walked over to Billy.

'I sure am curious to know why you're here, feller. I'm getting real impatient for Rick to turn up.

It was just after dark when Rick arrived. He rode in with a pack-horse loaded with provisions. Pete met him outside, and when he came into the shack with Pete, he looked Billy over. He was a half-breed, heavily built, with black hair, and a deep scar running from the corner of his eye down his right cheek. It gave him a sinister look.

'So this is the man who won't talk,' he said. 'Glad you kept him alive till I got back, Pete. I've got a few new tricks I want to try out, if the old ones don't work. But I've got to work on him outside in the daylight, so we'd better leave it till morning.'

'Right, Rick,' agreed Pete. 'Can't see that waiting another night will hurt. First thing, though. Sooner we know all about him, the better.'

'Maybe we won't have to wait,' suggested

Rick. 'After I've had some grub, I'm going to tell him exactly what I have in store for him. Maybe that'll change his mind.'

'I don't think so,' said Pete. 'I've got a feeling this kid's got grit.'

'We'll see,' said Rick, and proceeded to wolf down a large meal, with a complete absence of table manners. When he had finished, he belched loudly, got up, and walked over to Billy, taking his chair with him. He sat down in front of Billy, and belched again. The other three men watched with interest.

Rick eyed Billy for a few moments, without speaking. Billy returned his look. Then Rick spoke.

'Now, kid,' he said, 'I'm hoping, in a way, that what I tell you ain't going to change your mind, because there's nothing I like better than seeing a feller squirm. Maybe it's the Indian in me. But I figure Pete would sooner know now than tomorrow what you're doing here, so sing out any time you want to talk.

'What I'm going to tell you about, kid,' he went on, 'is the game I like to play most with a feller like you. It ain't ever failed yet, but if it did, I've got others to try out. It's an Indian torture rite they put young Indians through. First, I'll make four cuts in your back, near the shoulders, so that I can skewer two pegs in, under the flesh. Then I'll tie a rope to the pegs, and we'll hoist you up so's your feet are off the ground. There's a couple of high posts standing outside we can use for that. We'll lay another post along the top. And if that don't make you too uncomfortable,' he went on, his eyes lighting up in anticipation, 'we can always hang a few bags of stones on your feet.'

He paused for a few moments, then spoke again.

'You ready to talk now?''he asked.

'No,' answered Billy. Although his flesh was crawling, he managed to keep his face impassive.

'Good,' said Rick. 'I'm looking forward to the morning, then.'

Billy slept only fitfully that night, bound as he was, and with the thought of the following morning on his mind. He was

181

lying awake, just as dawn was breaking, when he heard the sound of gunfire. It sounded as if it could be coming from the lookout's position. Then there was silence. The four rustlers in the shack dressed hurriedly, put on their gun-belts, picked up their rifles, and after looking out to check that there was no-one in the immediate vicinity of the shack, they ran out. After they had left, there was sporadic gunfire for about twenty minutes. Then came a bloodcurdling scream, and the shooting finally stopped.

Billy heard a soft footfall outside the shack. Then the door burst open, and an Indian brave ran in, with rifle raised. He pointed the rifle at Billy, then saw that he was bound. He stepped forward, and for a few moments he looked into Billy's face.

'Billy Dare!' he said, and as two more Indians entered the shack, he spoke to them, and waved them back. Billy stared at the Indian. Then recognition came. He looked at the Indian's right side. It was scarred just above the waist. It was Little Hawk, the wounded Comanche he had helped when he was riding south through the Indian Territory on the trail of Hoffman and Pearce.

'Little Hawk!' he replied.

Little Hawk pulled out his knife, and cut the ropes around Billy's wrists and ankles. Billy rose, and flexed his arms and legs for a few moments. Then he took his gunbelt and Peacemaker from a peg on the wall, and strapped it on. Little Hawk made no move to stop him. Two more Comanches came into the shack, and stared at Billy. Little Hawk, who appeared to be the leader, spoke to them, and motioned to Billy to go outside. As he came out into the open, Billy could see that the valley contained a herd of a few hundred head. Several Indians were standing near the herd. He could see the bodies of four of the rustlers, and further back, towards the canyon, he could see the bodies of three Indians on the ground. He guessed that the fifth rustler had been killed at the lookout position. He thought quickly.

'I thank Little Hawk for his help,' he said. 'These cows (he motioned towards the herd) have been stolen from my brother across the river in Texas. I must take them back to him. I have promised. But because Little Hawk has helped me, he can take forty cows for his people.'

He hesitated, then opened his hands, fingers and thumbs outstretched, four times.

'Little Hawk could take *all* the cows,' suggested the Indian.

'Before Little Hawk can take all the cows, he will have to kill Billy Dare,' replied Billy.

For several moments Little Hawk pondered, his eyes on Billy. Then he spoke.

'Little Hawk no want to kill Billy Dare,' he said. 'Billy Dare saved his life. If Little Hawk helps to take cows back to Billy Dare's brother, how many cows can he have?'

Billy thought for a moment. He hadn't anticipated this offer of help.

'Fifty,' he replied, once again indicating the quantity in sign language. 'And you will take the horses of these men.' He pointed to the dead rustlers.

'Little Hawk agrees,' said the Indian. 'Little Hawk and Red Wolf will go with Billy Dare.'

During the day, Billy buried the bodies of the dead rustlers, and the Comanches drove off the fifty head, made up of twenty-five Box R and twenty-five Circle T cows, and the horses. They took their dead with them. Little Hawk and Red Wolf stayed behind.

The following morning they set off early with the herd. They took along the packhorse, with some of the provisions which had arrived with Rick. The two Comanches had removed their war paint. They had driven the herd about three miles in a south-easterly direction, heading for the Red River, when Billy saw two riders coming towards them. As they drew closer, Billy could see that both wore a Deputy US Marshal's badge. They held up their hands, and Billy signalled to the Indians to stop the herd. He rode over to the two lawmen. They were looking at the two Comanches in astonishment.

'Damndest thing I ever did see,' mar-
velled the older of the two deputies.
'Comanches working for a white man
on a trail-drive! Where are you taking
this beef?'

'Back to the Circle T and Box R
ranches in Texas, where they came from,'
replied Billy. 'These are stolen cattle.
Didn't you get a message from Sheriff
Lang in Grafton, asking you to watch
out for stolen cattle being held somewhere
around here?'

'Yes, we did,' agreed the deputy, 'just
before we set off from Fort Smith.'

He walked over to the herd, and
inspected a few brands. Then he came
back to Billy.

'What's your name?' he asked.

'Billy Dare,' replied Billy.

'It all lines up,' said the deputy. 'We
got word you might be around.'

'What happened to the rustlers?' enquired the second deputy.

Billy thought that a little bending of the
truth might be advisable.

'It was like this,' he said. 'Soon after I

186

got into the Indian Territory, I ran into Little Hawk over there, and a few of his braves. I first met Little Hawk a while back. Found him near the Kansas border with a head wound, and a bullet-hole in the side. Never did find out who shot him. I stopped the bleeding, and looked after him until his friends came looking for him. He figures he owes me a favour.

'Anyway,' went on Billy, 'Little Hawk offered to help me find those cattle. After a while, we came on a likely place, a valley with a lookout posted near the entrance. I sneaked down into it alone after dark, just to check the brands. I found they were the cattle I was after, but the rustlers caught me before I could get back to Little Hawk. Just about dawn, Little Hawk came into the valley after me. All five of the rustlers were killed, and three Indians.'

The two deputies seemed to be satisfied with his story. They nodded, and turned to leave. Then the older one turned back.

'Those two Comanches going right to the Circle T with you?' he asked.

'Yes,' replied Billy.

'Then maybe I'd better give you a letter explaining just what they are doing out of the Territory,' said the deputy.

He scrawled a few lines on a piece of paper, and handed it to Billy.

'Good luck,' he said, and rode off with his partner.

When the herd reached the Red River crossing-point which Murdoch had told Billy about, there was time enough to get them over before dark. They crossed without incident, and bedded the herd down. The next morning they headed for the Circle T.

During the remainder of the drive, Billy had an opportunity to observe the expert horsemanship of the Comanche. Perhaps a little ungainly on his feet, he was in his element on horseback. Little Hawk and Red Wolf had good horses, both geldings, and Billy remembered Seth Parker, the old army scout at Larraby, telling him that the Comanche was one of the best breeders of horses among the Indian tribes.

Back on the Circle T, it was a quiet morning. The air was still. Lois and Dan

Sinclair were walking from the corral back to the ranch-house, when they paused, and listened. From the north, out on the range, a faint drumming sound gradually increased in intensity. Looking towards it, they could see a rider in the distance, racing towards them at the maximum speed of which his mount was capable. He was waving his hat wildly in the air. As the sound of racing hoofbeats increased in volume, Dan recognized the rider.

'That's Jed!' he shouted. 'And he's going to kill that horse if he ain't careful.'

Moments later, the horse slid to a stop in front of Dan and Lois, and Jed leapt to the ground.

'You'll never believe this, Mr Sinclair,' he cried. 'Billy's back with the stolen cattle. He's on the north range. And he's got a couple of Comanches helping him!'

'What!' yelled Dan. 'Get me a horse!'

'Me too!' cried Lois.

'And tell two men to get saddled up, and come along with us,' ordered Dan.

When they reached the herd, Billy came to meet them.

'Welcome back, Billy,' said Lois.

'That goes for me too,' said Dan, 'and I'm mighty curious to find out how you managed to hire a couple of Comanches as trail-hands.'

'It's a long story,' said Billy. 'I'll tell you all about it later. Meantime, I've got to say goodbye to Little Hawk and Red Wolf over there. If it hadn't been for Little Hawk and his braves, I wouldn't be here now. I gave him fifty head of cattle. Didn't have any option really. You'll know why when I tell you the story later. I made a rough check on the herd on the way here, and I figure there are just under three hundred Circle T cows, and about a hundred Box R cows.' He walked over to the Indians, and spoke to Little Hawk.

'My brother Dan Sinclair thanks Little Hawk for his help,' he said.

'Now I go back to my people,' said Little Hawk. He raised his arm in salute. The two Indians wheeled their horses, and headed north.

Dan called Jed over.

'You and the boys cut out the Box R

cattle,' he ordered, 'and tomorrow you can drive them onto the Box R range.'

When Billy got back to the ranch-house with Lois and Dan, there was no sign of Mary.

'Where's Mary?' he enquired.

'Just after you left, she took a notion to visit a friend of hers back east,' answered Lois. 'She has a standing invitation. Don't know when she'll be back.'

They sat down, and Billy gave them the details of his recent mission.

'That's quite an experience you've had, Billy,' remarked Lois, when he had finished. 'What an evil man that half-breed was.'

'Well, thanks to Little Hawk, he won't do any more torturing,' commented Billy. He turned to Dan.

'Mr Sinclair,' he said, 'I was a mite worried about giving fifty head of somebody else's cattle to Little Hawk, but he did save my hide, and I figured it was the only thing I could do. By the way,' he went on, 'that fifty head was made up of twenty-five Box R and twenty-five Circle

T cows, but I found out later that there were a lot more Circle T cows than there were Box R, so you'll have to sort that out with the Box R.'

'Billy!' exclaimed Dan. 'You don't have any idea of how glad I am to get any cows back at all. Fifty head was a mighty cheap price to pay. And that other thing you mentioned, I'll sort it out with the Box R.'

Billy brought up a matter which was uppermost in his mind.

'You remember,' he said, 'that I told you I heard those rustlers say that Hoffman and Pearce were riding back to the Diamond S. Did anyone see them when they got back?'

'Yes,' replied Dan. 'They turned up a few days after you left. They were spotted riding in from the north, and there was an ambush waiting for them, but something made them suspicious, and there was a shoot-out. Pearce was killed, but Hoffman escaped.'

'Do they know which way he went?' enquired Billy.

'A posse took off after him,' said Dan, 'but I don't know how they got on. You'd better ride into town and ask the sheriff, if he's there.'

'This means,' observed Billy, 'that I've only got one killer to chase now. But I think that Hoffman is the worst of the three. I've got a feeling that he's the one who strangled my mother. I'll go into town in the morning.'

'I'm glad, Billy,' said Lois, 'that the odds against you aren't so high now. It almost seems as if fate is taking a hand.'

'Maybe,' said Billy. 'But I still aim to give fate a helping hand. The longer Hoffman is on the loose, the more harm he can do.'

The next morning, Billy found Sheriff Lang in his office. He told him of the events in the Indian Territory, including his meeting with the two deputy marshals.

'You did a good job there, Billy,' the sheriff remarked, when he had finished. 'You heard about Hoffman and Pearce?'

'Yes,' replied Billy. 'Mr Sinclair told me. Did you manage to track Hoffman down?'

'No such luck,' replied the sheriff. 'We were pretty close on his heels at the start, but somehow he managed to give us the slip. But I'm sure he was heading north. I reckon that he's holed up in the Indian Territory.

'You know, Billy,' he went on, 'not long ago, the Indian Territory was just for the Indians. Then the stagecoach routes and the railroads cut across the Territory, and the gamblers, prostitutes and criminals moved in. Nowadays it's a safe haven for any outlaw who's been operating outside, and wants to stay out of sight until things quieten down. That's why I think Hoffman is in the Indian Territory. And if he is, he's pretty certain to be with the Williams gang he used to ride with. There's a strong rumour that they have a hideout somewhere near to Red Rock, though the law has never been able to find it. Anyhow, I've notified the US Marshal in Fort Smith that Hoffman is probably in the Indian Territory, and there's nothing more I can do.'

When Billy got back to the Circle T, he

told Dan and Lois what he had learned from the sheriff. He also told them that he was returning to the Indian Territory to search for Hoffman.

9

After Billy had taken his leave of Lois and Dan the following morning, he headed for Red Rock, a small town well up into the Indian Territory. He hoped that Sheriff Lang had been right when he guessed that Hoffman might be in that vicinity. In any case, there were no other leads to follow.

Red Rock turned out to be a stagecoach station plus saloon, hotel, store, and a few dwellings. Billy stopped at the hotel, dismounted, and went in. There was no-one at the desk. He punched the bell. A man appeared, and gave Billy a searching look.

'You got a room?' asked Billy.

'Number six,' said the man, handing the key over. 'Sign the book.' He expertly twirled the register round in front of Billy. Billy put his name in it, and twirled it back. As Billy climbed the stairs, he looked back. The man was peering closely at the entry.

Billy relaxed for half an hour on the bed. Then he went down, and took his horse over to the livery stable, which was tacked onto the stagecoach station. As he led his horse into the stable, a man came out of the stagecoach office, and followed him into the stable. He was a dapper, pleasant-looking man in his fifties.

'You want to leave that horse here?' he asked.

'Yes,' replied Billy. 'I'm waiting in Red Rock for a friend. Don't know for how long. Maybe he's got held up somewhere. We aim to head for Texas, and find a job punching cows.'

'I'm Brinkel,' said the man. 'I'm the stagecoach agent, and I run the livery stable here as well.'

'Billy Dare,' said Billy. 'If you've got things to do, I'll tend to my horse myself. He gets kind of upset if I leave it to anybody else.'

'I know what you mean,' smiled Brinkel, a lover of horses himself. 'Water's over there, feed's over there, and put him in that corner on the right. I'm going back to the office. Got a few things to finish off in there. Call in when you're finished.'

When Billy called in later at the agent's office, he found Brinkel seated at his desk.

'Have a seat,' invited Brinkel. 'I've been wondering,' he went on, 'whether you'd like a job here while you're waiting for your friend. I could do with some help in the livery stable. You could bunk down in the stable if you want. There's a little room at the back, with a bunk in it. How does that strike you?'

'Thanks for the offer,' said Billy gratefully, deciding that he could trust Brinkel. 'That'll suit me fine. But before you take me on, I think I should tell you my real reason for being here. Fact is, I'm after an outlaw called Hoffman, who might be holed up with the Williams gang somewhere around here.'

He showed Brinkel the 'wanted' poster, and pointed to Hoffman's picture.

'That's him,' he said. 'Have you seen

him around here lately?'

Brinkel studied the picture closely, and read the description.

'Not lately,' he replied, 'but he looks like a man I saw here a couple of times two or three years ago. I remember him because he had an argument with another man out in the street there, and near beat him to death. You a lawman?' he asked.

'No,' replied Billy. 'This is personal. Hoffman murdered my mother. Did you ever hear that the Williams gang have a hideout somewhere near here?'

'I've heard strong rumours about that,' replied Brinkel, 'but nothing definite. I think the rumours are probably true, but I've got no idea at all just where that hideout might be.'

'Looks like I've got to hang around here hoping that Hoffman will show up,' said Billy, resignedly.

'If Hoffman's near here, he'll come into Red Rock sometime,' said Brinkel. 'It's just a matter of waiting till he turns up. There are badmen coming here all the time. They're all over the Territory. I

199

can tell you, the stage hold-ups we get in the Indian Territory are a real headache. We've got a man riding shotgun on every stage just now.'

The next morning, Billy moved out of the hotel. As he paid his bill, he spoke to the man at the desk.

'Come out here to give Mr Brinkel a hand,' he said. 'I'll be bunking down in the stable.'

Billy quickly settled down to his work at the stable. Most of his duties were similar to those he had carried out at Ellsworth, but since Red Rock was a relay station on the stagecoach route, this meant extra work when a stagecoach came in, as the horses had to be replaced by fresh ones, and the replaced ones had to be tended to. Brinkel was grateful for his help.

'Wish you were here permanent,' he said to Billy, after he had been there for a few days. 'You've no idea how good it is to talk to somebody you can trust. A lot of the townsfolk here favour the outlaws, and when the lawmen do show up, they don't give them any help at all.'

'Why don't you have a lawman in town?' asked Billy.

'Because Congress decided that the law over the whole of the Indian Territory had to be enforced from Fort Smith, Arkansas,' explained Brinkel, 'and I reckon it just ain't possible to do it that way. Not properly, anyway. Some day, we'll have local law enforcement officers like they have outside the Territory, but when that day will come is hard to say.'

During the next week, whenever he could spare the time, and with Brinkel's agreement, Billy rode out from Red Rock for ten miles or so, in a different direction each time. He was hoping to see something which might give him a lead as to where the Williams gang was holed up, but so far he had been unsuccessful.

Then, one day around noon, three deputy marshals rode into Red Rock. They came to see Brinkel in his office. Brinkel called Billy in.

'They've decided in Fort Smith,' said the leader of the deputies, whose name was Greenall, 'that something's got to be done about the Williams gang. They've been rampaging around the Indian Territory, holding up stagecoaches and robbing trains for far too long. Everybody's complaining about it. The marshal in Fort Smith has got your Company to agree to send out a decoy stagecoach on a normal scheduled run across the Territory. The coach wouldn't carry paying passengers, but deputy marshals dressed as ordinary passengers might be, and wearing no badges. The driver and shotgun rider would be deputy marshals as well.'

Brinkel interrupted.

'But how can you be reasonably sure that the stage would be held up?' he queried.

'I was coming to that,' replied Greenall, 'and that's why we're here. Is there anybody around here you think might be helping those outlaws?'

'Several,' replied Brinkel, 'but only one that I'm reasonably sure about. That's a man called Hall. He lives in a shack on the edge of town. He's been seen around with some shady-looking characters from time to time. He ain't got a regular job, but always seems to have plenty of money for drinking and gambling. I see him going in the saloon there most afternoons.'

'He sounds like the man we're looking for,' said Greenall. 'Now, without telling anybody direct, we would want the gang to learn that a westbound stage is carrying a large consignment of banknotes through the Territory. And we'd want to do it without the gang suspecting that we'd fed them the information.'

'That's not going to be easy,' muttered Brinkel. 'The Williams gang ain't no fools.' His brow wrinkled as he considered and rejected several possible plans which came to his mind.

Billy had been thinking as well.

'I've got an idea,' he said. 'You could call Hall into the office as he's passing on the way to the saloon, and get him to sit on the other side of the desk from you. Then you could tell him I'm leaving soon, and ask him if he knows anybody who might take my job permanent. Say you're asking him because he knows everybody around town.'

He walked over to the door, opened it, went through the doorway, leaving it half-open, and stopped outside.

'Now look,' he said, 'with the door half-open like it is now, I can see you at the desk, Mr Brinkel, but if Hall was sitting in the other chair, I wouldn't be able to see him. So what I could do,' he went on, 'would be to come up to the door, half open it, and say something like "Mr Brinkel—about that big consignment of banknotes on the westbound stage a week next Friday. Will the..." Then I would pretend to notice, sudden like, that somebody else was in the office, and I would break off and leave. You think that might work?' he asked.

'That's a good plan, Billy,' said Brinkel, turning to Greenall.

'What do you think?' he asked. 'A good plan,' agreed Greenall. 'I think it has a good chance of working if you act it right. Now the next thing we have to do,' he went on, 'is to settle on the date we're going to run the coach. There's a scheduled westward run crossing the eastern border of the Territory on the sixteenth of this month, that's two weeks from tomorrow. If we run the decoy coach on that date, that should give us enough time to get things organized. Would you check that that date is agreed by your Company, Mr Brinkel?'

'I'll do that,' said Brinkel.

'That means,' went on Greenall, 'that if we stick to that date, you've got to give that false information to Hall by a week tomorrow at the latest, so that he has time to get the information to the Williams gang in time for them to plan the raid.'

'I'll call Hall in as soon as I've got the go-ahead from the Company,' promised Brinkel.

'The planning is up to us,' said Greenall, 'but just so as you'll know, the driver will be a deputy who's done a good bit of stagecoach-driving before he took a deputy's job. There'll be four more deputies, one riding shotgun, and three inside. We could have done with four inside, but three was the most we could manage.'

'Will you take me in that coach, to make up the four?' asked Billy. 'I think that there is an outlaw Hoffman with the Williams gang. He murdered my mother early this year, and I've been trying to catch up with him ever since.'

'I'm very sorry, but I can't take you along,' replied Greenall. 'All the men on that stage have got to be men fully experienced in handling firearms. Otherwise it ain't fair to the rest.'

'I really would like to go on that stage, Mr Greenall,' persisted Billy. 'Would you mind coming outside for a few minutes?'

'Sure,' he said.

They walked out of the back door, followed by Brinkel and the other two deputies. Billy picked up four small cans from a pile lying outside. He placed them, several inches apart, on top of a fence near the livery stable. Then he went into the stable for his gunbelt. He buckled it on, and went outside. He stood facing the cans, about seven yards away.

'Call,' he asked Greenall.

'Now!' shouted Greenall.

Almost as if by magic, the Peacemaker appeared in Billy's right hand, and four shots followed, so closely spaced that they almost merged into one. Four tin-cans jerked backwards, and fell to the ground.

Brinkel whistled under his breath. The deputies looked at one another.

'We'll be glad to have you along,' said Greenall. 'We'll deputize you for the job. As soon as the date is confirmed, you can arrange to head east, to join the stagecoach at the border. The deputies will be on it. Of course, we don't know where the gang will hit; most likely it will be nearer Red Rock than the border. All the same, you'd better play safe, and join us at the border.

'Since you'll be coming along,' he continued, 'let me give you some idea of how we aim to play this. On the way, everybody will keep a sharp lookout for the gang. The deputies inside the coach will have field-glasses, which should help. When the gang are spotted, and just before they're in shooting-distance, the driver will stop the coach, and he and the shotgun rider will get ready to fire on the gang.'

The deputies rode off for Fort Smith the following morning. Before they left, Brinkel told them that he would ask the stagecoach company to make arrangements directly with Fort Smith for the use of a stagecoach for the project. Approval of the plan by the Company reached Brinkel three days later. The same day, in the afternoon, he watched out for Hall passing on his way to the saloon, and called him in. Billy saw Hall enter the office, and he and Brinkel carried out the plan which Billy had proposed. Billy went into the office after Hall had left.

'It worked!' said Brinkel, 'I'm sure of it. Just for a second his eyes lit up when you mentioned those banknotes. Then he pretended he hadn't heard. He said he'd ask around to see if anybody was interested in the job here.'

The following week, Billy took the eastbound coach to a small town on the eastern border of the Territory, to rendezvous with the decoy coach, which arrived at the scheduled time. Three of the deputies on the coach were the ones who had recently been in Red Rock. The remaining two were acting as driver and shotgun rider. Greenall, the leader of the deputies, greeted Billy, and introduced him to the two deputies he had not already met.

'We heard that Hall has taken the bait,' he said.

'Yes,' said Billy. 'Mr Brinkel's certain of it.'

'Good,' said Greenall. 'Let's get moving.'

They climbed aboard, and headed west, maintaining a constant lookout, and making all the scheduled stops. It was not until they were fifteen miles east of Red Rock that they noticed anything suspicious. One of the deputies spotted a group of riders well ahead, and only visible through glasses, close to a small copse of trees to the left of, and a little way back from, the road.

'Looks like six riders,' he reported.

As the stagecoach drew nearer to it, the

group of riders moved behind the trees out of sight.

'Get ready,' ordered Greenall. He leaned out of the coach and spoke to the driver. 'We've spotted them,' he shouted. 'Six of them, ahead on the left. Stop the coach on open ground if you can.'

As the stagecoach drew abreast of them, the gang broke from cover, and headed towards it. The six of them were all masked. As the stagecoach proceeded, the gang fell in behind it, and started to overhaul it. As the six riders got closer, Billy could see that one of them was a big man, over six feet tall. As the stagecoach driver pulled the horses up, and he and his companion got ready to fire, the gang divided, three riders heading for each side of the stagecoach from behind.

The reception the robbers got was entirely unexpected by them. They were suddenly faced with Billy and five officers of the law, hand-picked for their courage, and with a proven fighting ability. Within seconds, five of the robbers were out of action. The big man was a little behind the rest, and still behind the coach when the lawmen started shooting. Seeing five of the gang hit, he wheeled his horse, and rode off at full speed. The deputies fired after him, but he did not appear to be hit.

When the shooting stopped, three of the robbers were dead, and two severely wounded. The wounded ones were quickly disarmed. The deputies escaped lightly. Two of them had a flesh wound in the arm, and a third had some wood splinters in his face. Billy, Greenall and the other deputy were unhurt.

Greenall spoke to his men.

'Take the two wounded robbers into Red Rock,' he ordered. 'The dead ones can be picked up later.'

He turned to Billy.

'And you and me will go after the big one,' he said. 'Do you figure he might be Hoffman?'

'I'm sure of it,' replied Billy.

Billy and Greenall mounted two of the outlaws' horses which had remained nearby, and headed in the direction Hoffman had taken. They caught sight of him in the distance almost immediately. Then he disappeared from view. They followed, catching sight of him from time to time, and gaining slightly. Then, after they had not seen him for a while, Greenall stopped.

'I don't like this,' he said. 'We should have spotted him again before now. I wouldn't put it past Hoffman to try and ambush us.'

Just as he finished speaking, a rifle-bullet passed close to Billy's ear, and they both rode hastily for cover behind a large boulder standing at the bottom of a rocky slope. They dismounted.

'Did you see where that came from?' asked Greenall.

'No,' answered Billy.

Then a second bullet struck the rock face behind them, as they sheltered behind the boulder.

'Well, he's got us pinned down for now,' observed Greenall, 'but he can't get a direct shot at us in here without showing himself.'

A few seconds passed. Then a third shot

hit the rock face behind them, and the bullet ricocheted off, whined past Billy's nose, and ploughed a shallow furrow across the forehead of Greenall, who fell to the ground. Billy poked his arm around the side of the boulder, and fired a few shots in the direction he thought the rifle-shots had come from. Then he went back to have a look at Greenall. The bullet-mark ran right across his forehead. It was bleeding slightly. As Billy inspected the wound, Greenall shook his head, opened his eyes, and sat up groggily.

'I can't see,' he groaned.

'Just a minute,' said Billy. 'I'll wipe that blood away.'

'It ain't that,' said Greenall, a hint of panic in his voice. 'My eyes ain't working.'

Billy looked at him with some concern.

'In that case,' he said, 'as soon as we're sure Hoffman's gone, I'll get you back to Red Rock. Maybe the doctor there can help.'

It was now growing dark, and there had been no further fire from Hoffman.

They felt sure that if he hadn't already left, he would do so soon. They stayed where they were until morning. Greenall's sight did not return during the night, and at first light Billy helped him onto his horse, took hold of the reins, mounted the other horse, and headed for Red Rock.

About a week after his return to Red Rock with Greenall, Billy was occupied in the livery stable one afternoon. The deputies, including Greenall, had left for Fort Smith with their prisoners. Greenall had had occasional flashes of vision since he returned to Red Rock, and was hopeful that his sight would soon be permanently restored. Billy was wondering if there was any point in him staying on in Red Rock, now that the gang had received such a crushing blow. With most of its members either dead or in custody, Hoffman had probably left the area. He decided to stay on three more days, then leave.

He had just reached this decision, when he happened to glance out of the stable entrance into the street beyond. He saw a bearded man, big enough to be Hoffman, enter the store.

He buckled on his gunbelt, with the holstered Peacemaker, walked out into the street, and leaned against a hitching-rail a few yards from the store entrance, waiting.

A few minutes later, the bearded man opened the door of the store. He paused in the doorway, and looked up and down the street, his eyes passing over Billy. He emerged, and turned towards the saloon. As he did so, Billy saw, quite clearly, the notch in the man's right ear.

The man started walking towards the saloon, with his back to Billy. Billy straightened up from the hitching-rail, and took a sideways step into the street.

'Hoffman!' he called.

The man stopped. His hand moved near to his gun handle. He slowly turned to face Billy. He looked Billy over, then visibly relaxed.

'Who are you?' he asked.

Face to face at last with his mother's murderer, Billy forced himself to speak calmly.

'My name is Billy Dare,' he said. 'I want you to think back to one morning early this year. You and two friends of yours called in at a homestead near Larraby in East Texas. My mother was on her own there. You beat her up, and then strangled her and took her savings.'

Hoffman looked up and down the street. It was deserted.

'I remember,' he said. 'You aiming to do something about it?'

'I know that your two friends are both dead,' said Billy, 'so there's only you left now, Hoffman. I'm going to kill you.'

Hoffman sneered. Looking at Billy, he felt no doubt about his own ability to outgun this youngster. But Billy's calmness and self-assurance irritated him. He decided he'd like to see his young opponent rattled, before eliminating him.

'Before you try killing me,' he said to Billy, 'maybe you'd like to hear about your mother. When I started roughing her up because she wouldn't tell us where the money was hidden, she started calling "Billy!", but we knew there was no Billy around. And when I was tightening that bandanna around her throat, she was still trying to call "Billy!", but all that was coming out was a sort of gurgle. It sounded so funny, I had to laugh.'

With a superhuman effort, Billy suppressed the feeling of blind rage which threatened to engulf him.

Not detecting any visible response from Billy, Hoffman decided to end the confrontation.

He continued:

'And when I tightened up on that bandanna a bit more...'

He stopped in mid-sentence, and his hand flashed to his gun handle. Billy scarcely seemed to move, but suddenly there was a single puff of smoke from his right side, and a hole appeared in Hoffman's vest, over the heart. Hoffman had not fired. As he staggered backwards, for a brief moment his face registered a look of utter astonishment. Then his legs crumpled, and he fell to the ground.

Billy holstered the Peacemaker. Suddenly he felt a great relief, as though a huge weight had been lifted from his mind. He had reached the end of the vengeance trail. The next morning, after breakfast, he took his leave of Brinkel, mounted the bay, and headed for the Circle T.

This Large Print Book for the Partially sighted, who cannot read normal print, is published under the auspices of

THE ULVERSCROFT FOUNDATION

THE ULVERSCROFT FOUNDATION

. . . we hope that you have enjoyed this Large Print Book. Please think for a moment about those people who have worse eyesight problems than you . . . and are unable to even read or enjoy Large Print, without great difficulty.

You can help them by sending a donation, large or small to:

**The Ulverscroft Foundation,
1, The Green, Bradgate Road,
Anstey, Leicestershire, LE7 7FU,
England.**

or request a copy of our brochure for more details.

The Foundation will use all your help to assist those people who are handicapped by various sight problems and need special attention.

Thank you very much for your help.

Other DALES Western Titles In Large Print

ELLIOT CONWAY
The Dude

JOHN KILGORE
Man From Cherokee Strip

J. T. EDSON
Buffalo Are Coming

ELLIOT LONG
Savage Land

HAL MORGAN
The Ghost Of Windy Ridge

NELSON NYE
Saddle Bow Slim